New Orleans

Mysteries

O'Neil De Noux

For Calixte and Louise

TABLE OF CONTENTS

All Stories *Copyright* © O'Neil De Noux

Maria's Hand
 first appeared on *Amazon Shorts* (**www.amazon.com**), 2006

The Gold Bug of Jean Lafitte
 first appeared in *The Mammoth Book of Historical Erotica*, 1999

Guilty of Dust and Sin
 first appeared on *Amazon Shorts* (**www.amazon.com**), 2005

The Desire Streetcar
 first appeared in *Pulphouse Fiction Spotlight* Magazine, Issue 2, 1992

A Heartbeat
 first appeared *Dead of Night* Magazine, Issue 11, 1995

The Man With Moon Hands
 first appeared in *New Mystery* Magazine, Issue 3, 1992

Bet the Devil
 first appeared in *A Shot in the Dark* Magazine, Issue 10, 1997

The Portrait of Lenore
 first appeared in *Whispering Willow Mysteries* Anthology Dagger Edition, 1997

Except for the Ghosts
 first appeared in a SPECIAL EDITION of *Land's End* Catalog (United Kingdom and Germany), 2000

So Napoleon Almost Slept here, Right?
 first appeared in *The Mammoth Book of Future Cops* Anthology, 2003

A good editor tells writers, "Let the story speak for itself." If you write a good story, it'll be accepted (OK, that's an over-simplification because editorial selection is very subjective). What an editor doesn't want is a lot of explanation of what the story's about. Let the story speak for itself. That's what I intend to do here, however, I'd like to talk a little about my town.

New Orleans is America's *eternal city*, as Rome is to Europeans. Built where no city should have been built — six feet below sea level, completely surrounded by water, on a floating land mass that oozes beneath us as it sinks buildings and cracks streets — for over two hundred and ninety-years years it has battled mother nature who simply wants her swamp back.

When Frenchman Jean Baptiste le Moyne – Sieur de Bienville, along with Major Paillous de Barbezan, six carpenters, four Canadians and thirty convicted salt smugglers who'd been sent to Louisiana in lieu of jail, decided here is where they'd build their capital city, New Orleans has struggled to survive, withstanding fires, epidemics of malaria, yellow fever and cholera, as well as hurricanes, Yankees and the British. In that first year, 1718, a fierce hurricane knocked down most of the buildings.

Beside that big bitch *Katrina* in 2005, south Louisiana has been ravaged by forty-nine hurricanes since 1851, including *major storms* in 1779, 1879, 1887, 1893, 1901, 1909, 1915, 1926, 1947, 1948, 1965, 1969, 1998. That doesn't include flooding from the Mississippi River (thirty-eight major floods between 1735 and 1827) tropical storms and innumerable floods from heavy rains.

France ceded the city to Spain in 1762, then took it back in 1803, only to sell it and all of its people to the United States. Fire destroyed half the city in 1788 and then the other half in 1794. In 1815, the British sent a crack army to take the city and were stopped by a ragtag army of Creoles, free men of color, pirates, Kentucky and Tennessee militia, backwoodsmen, Choctaw volunteers, fortified by a limited number of U.S. army regulars, U.S. sailors and Marines and led by a general whose only experience was fighting insurgent native American tribes.

Yankees took the city in 1862. Reconstruction helped retard the city's growth, exascerbating the long-held belief by New Orleanians to grab life while it was around, let the good times roll, and bedamned building a city that actually worked. Yet, New Orleans survived.

And therein lies the dissonance – tension and clash resulting from combing two disharmonious or unsuitable elements – rich and poor, educated and uneducated, hard times and good times. A recent survey listed the world's cities with the highest per-capita murder rate. First was Kabul and second Bagdad (cities mired in war). The third? You guessed it. New Orleans. Its nothing new. In the Nineteenth Century one newspaper described the city as 'hell on earth' with bodies lying in gutters. The Americans have tried to tame her. It took the US Navy (during World War I) to close Storyville, the infamous red-light district at the edge of the French Quarter.

Violence is no stranger to a city that has had to fight for its existance since its creation. So it's no mystery that New Orleans is mysterious.

Maria's Hand

Monday, 15 June 1891

The man on the beat was waiting for Dugas at the Tenth Precinct station house with the trunk with the woman's hand inside.

"Ah, you must be our detective," the patrolman said as Dugas stepped from the police boat to the station house dock, "I'm Donahoe. Joe Donahoe." The big man extended his hand to shake which Dugas missed and fell back on the boat, twisting his left ankle as his leg hit a guide rail. He winced and climbed off without assistance, his ankle burning now.

Patrolman Donahoe was pushing forty and burly with thick sandy hair and a matching moustache, along with a reddish drinker's nose. He'd left his sky blue bowler inside the station, his sky blue New Orleans police shirt streaked with sweat as he wiped his brow with a gray handkerchief.

"Come on in." Donahoe turned and went into the new wood-frame station house built along the New Basin Canal for the ten patrolmen responsible for the thinly-settled district at the rear of the city which ran all the way to Lake Pontchartrain.

Detective Jacques Dugas — six feet tall, one hundred seventy pounds with dark brown eyes, wore his dark brown hair parted down the middle and his moustache neatly trimmed. Twenty-six years old, he was young for a detective. A French-American, he was one of the few non-Irishmen on the job. Today he wore a lightweight blue suit.

A elderly man with a thick shock of gray hair, a matching unkempt beard and skin so dark it looked blue-black, sat on a bench across from the desk sergeant's high counter. Wearing a long coat over several layers of shirts, well-worn dungarees and work boots, it was obvious the old man was living rough on the down-and-out.

Donahoe led the way around the counter to a desk, Dugas limping slightly. The trunk was a brown portmanteau, nearly three feet long, two feet high, with a thick handle atop between two snap-locks which had been forced open.

"Look inside," Donahoe said, folding his arms.

Dugas peeked in and saw the hand resting atop a pile of clothes. It didn't look real, more like a manikin's, whitish-pink in color, long nails painted bright red. It was a left hand, a thin wedding band on its ring finger; the hand had been severed just above the wrist in what looked like one neat cut.

"Fella over there brought it in after breaking open the locks," Donahoe's voice had the typical copper's accusatory tone, "claims he found it on the side of the road."

Dugas looked at the elderly man, "What's your name?"

"Homer Jones, suh."

"What road?" Dugas gingerly moved around the counter.

"Bayou Road, suh." The man staring at his limp.

Dugas took out his note pad and pencil as he sat on the bench next to Homer. He'd already written the date and time he'd received the call and quickly jotted his time of arrival, glancing up at the clock on the wall, seeing it was nine-ten a.m., then wrote Donahoe's name and the name Homer Jones.

He jotted 'Bayou Road' and then asked, "When did you find it?"

"This mornin' just after sunup. It was 'tween the road and the bayou like someone just 'trew and missed the water. I tried not to break the locks. But I could feel somethin' inside ..."

And he wanted what was inside. Homer looked Dugas in the eyes with such sincerity, the way an innocent man looked a cop straight in the eyes, nothing to hide. He answered the next questions without hesitation. He'd seen no one in the area this morning. He lived in a shack, as he called it, up the road a ways closer to the lake. He was headed to mooch a hand-out from one of the kitchens along the 'back a town' — indicating the Faubourg St. John and the new residential Faubourg Pontchartrain being built on the marshy area between the city and the lake.

"I seen it had women's clothes and shoes. The hand was at the bottom and I didn't think it was real 'til I touch it. So I closed up the trunk and went lookin' for a copper. Didn't want to just leave the trunk there with a lady's hand inside."

"I searched him," said Donahoe. "Don't look like he stole anything from the trunk." A disapproving smirk on the copper's face now as Donahoe added, "He's just one of them bums camped up the bayou across from the park. We're in the process of rousting them for the developers."

Dugas to Homer, "Anyone you know lives near where you found the trunk?"

"No, suh. Most of our shacks are up the bayou."

Rubbing his ankle, Dugas closed his eyes and distracted himself with a vision of semi-rural Bayou Road, the oldest road in the entire area, an old Indian trail running alongside Bayou St. John, predating even the French.

"I intend to ask around," Homer said. "Maybe somebody seen somethin' and I can let you know."

Donahoe injected, "We don't need no bums investigatin' anything."

Dugas stood, nodding to Homer, before asking Donahoe, "You finished with him?"

"I guess so."

Leading Homer Jones outside, Dugas stopped him and leaned against the rail surrounding the low porch of the station. They had their backs to the station so Donahoe couldn't hear. Dugas kept his voice low as he handed Homer one of the new business cards his captain had distributed to all the detectives. "This has my name and how to get a hold of me. You can read, can't you?"

"Yes, suh. Mister Detective Dugas." Homer looking at the card now.

"I want you to do just as you suggested," Dugas said, reaching down to massage his ankle which was tightening up badly. "Ask around. People will talk to you when they won't talk to me."

"I know that. I seen a lot myself bein' around the old plantation all my life."

It took Dugas a second to realize, so he asked, "You used to work the Allard Plantation?" This large defunct plantation was now City Park, fifteen hundred acres just being developed into an urban park.

"Yes, suh. Born there in 1831. I was a field hand 'til the war came. Ran off and joined the Billy Yanks."

Dugas stared at the former slave who'd run off to join the U.S. Army during the Civil War. The old man's eyes got a troubled look in them. "I was wounded bad at the crater. Petersburg. June 30, 1864."

My God, thought Dugas, the Petersburg crater. Everyone knew the story, even Dugas who wasn't even born until after the war. Near the end of the war, during the siege of Petersburg, some enterprising army sappers had dug under the confederate lines and blew up an entire section of the breastworks, creating a huge crater. The Yankees sent in colored troops to swarm through the break in the line, only the crater was so big the rebels had time to recover before the troops could get out of the bowl, which became a shooting gallery.

"I tried to surrender," Homer said, as if following Dugas's thoughts. "But the Rebs would have none of that. Kept killin' everyone. I got shot three times and crawl out the back side and the Yankees pulled me clear. Lost all ma' friends that day. Every one of 'em."

Homer turned his brown eyes to Dugas. "Your Daddy fought in the war?"

Dugas shook his head. "I'm the first one in my family to speak English. During the war we remained Frenchmen, not about to fight for the Rebels or Yankees."

"Smart folks."

When Dugas shook the old man's hand, he slipped him a dollar and Homer thanked him kindly and walked off down the New Basin Canal. Back inside the station house, Donahoe was sitting behind the counter.

"You got quite a mystery on your hands, Det. Dugas."

Dugas hobbled back to the trunk.

"Hurt your leg?"

Dugas nodded as he lifted the hand out to examine it closely. No other wounds were visible and nothing beneath the fingernails. Victims often scratch their assailants, leaving skin under the nails. These were clean. He gently placed it on the table and pulled out the clothes, one piece at a time.

The skirt was linen with a matching jacket. The shoes were labeled "Made in NYC" and were size four. He found a laundry mark on a cream colored silk blouse that read: EKD LAUN.

"Think he cut it off when she was still alive?" Donahoe sat with his hands behind his head.

"Most likely post-mortem."

"Huh?"

"Few people would let someone cut their hand off without jerking. The wound's too neat."

Donahoe smiled for the first time but it wasn't a friendly one. "I heard 'a you. The Frenchie Detective. Everyone says you're pretty smart. You gonna need to be to solve this one." With that Donahoe picked up his bowler and walked out.

#

The coroner was 'fairly' confident the dismemberment was post-mortem. Dugas noted it in his notes, as well as the approximate time of dismemberment, within the last forty-eight hours and the approximate age of the victim, between twenty and thirty.

Leaving the portmanteau in the evidence locker at the Detective Bureau, Dugas took the blouse to the nearest laundry whose proprietor recognized the laundry mark and directed Dugas to the Edkins Laundry, adjacent to St. Louis #3 Cemetery on Esplanade Avenue.

Alighting slowly from the mule-drawn streetcar, Dugas stood with his weight on his right leg and looked across the avenue at Edkins Laundry, which occupied the bottom floor of a two-story wood frame house next to the white walls of the cemetery.

The owner-operator, a short squat man named Eldon Edkins recognized the blouse as owned by one of his regular customers, Maria Alcamo. Dugas asked for an address.

"She's the wife of the baker right down the street," Edkins pointed down Esplanade. "It's called Pane Fresco. The bakery."

"When was the last time you saw Mrs. Alcamo?"

Edkins checked his book and said, "Last Tuesday, the ninth."

"Was she with someone?"

"Someone. No. She always comes alone. Is she is trouble?"

Dugas shook his head and asked, "What does she look like?"

"Pretty." The man's eyes lit up. "Very pretty with dark hair and dark eyes. Italian, you know. Sort of sultry."

"What does her husband look like?"

"Him, I've never seen."

Mr. Alcamo was a big man, a good three inches taller tan Dugas's six-feet, and balding, a thick man with large arms. Clean shaven, he had deep-set green eyes and greeted Dugas with a warm smile from behind the counter. Pane Fresco, which Dugas knew meant 'fresh bread' in Italian, smelled of freshly baked bread and cinnamon and other spices, nutmeg most likely.

The smile went away when Dugas opened the lapel of his coat to show his gold N.O.P.D. star-and-crescent badge, then held up the blouse. The big man's face went from surprise to confusion to fear, as the man asked, "What has happened?"

Dugas asked to see his wife.

The big man's chin sank. "She no live here anymore. She left me. Just before Christmas." He looked at the blouse again as Dugas placed it atop the glass counter. Through quivering lips, he said, "Por favore, senoré policia … is Maria OK?"

Dugas just stared into the deep set eyes as they filled with tears.

"No. No," the man cried as his shoulders slumped and he broke down. An older woman came scrambling out of the back as

Alcamo lay his head on the counter and sobbed. In shrill Italian, too rapid for Dugas to follow, the woman was alternately trying to calm Alcamo and cursing Dugas, calling him a devil of dubious birth. Those phrases were easily identified. The old woman spotted the blouse and went suddenly quiet.

It was then Dugas noticed another woman standing in the doorway leading to the back of the bakery. She looked like a smaller version of the baker but still had all of her black hair. Eyeing Dugas she said, "I am Louisa. Who are you?"

Like her brother, Louisa Alcamo spoke excellent English. As the big man struggled to control his sobbing, Dugas learned from Louisa that Maria Alcamo was living the 'high life' since leaving her husband. "She hangs out in saloons. I think she's whoring it." Which sent the husband into another long sobbing tirade, the old woman, who turned out to be the baker's mother, rubbed his back and telling him, in Italian, to let it out.

"Which saloons?" Dugas.

"Take your pick. She ain't picky."

None of the Alcamos, who lived above the bakery, knew where Maria lived now, neither did any of the neighbors. By the time Dugas returned to the bakery, Mr. Alessio Alcamo was more composed. Dugas took the big baker to the Central Police Station to interview, getting him away from his mama and sister, getting him in a more controlled environment.

Before leaving, Dugas asked to look around the apartment and the bakery. If a body had been dismembered, they'd done a good job of cleaning up. The bakery and apartment were clean but not freshly scrubbed, which would have increased Dugas's suspicion.

"Do you have a picture of Maria I could borrow?"

Louisa brought a portrait of Maria to Dugas, telling him he could keep it. They had plenty as Maria was vain and had many pictures. It was a five by seven inch portrait of a very pretty young woman sitting in a chair. Maria's dark eyes stared right into the camera lens, her long hair pulled away from her lovely face with combs. Maria had a delicate nose and finely sculptured lips On second look, Dugas could see a mischievous glint in those dark eyes.

Turning the photo over Dugas was surprised no studio name was on back.

"Where did she have this picture taken?"

"Who knows?"

#

Perched on the small wooden chair in the tiny interview room of the Detective Bureau, Alessio Alcamo brought none of the hysterics with him. Leaning his large arms on the little table and staring Dugas in the eye, he answered every question directly, without hesitation. Dugas studied the man, focusing on the way he answered rather than his blanket denials. Alcamo hadn't seen Maria since January, when she came back briefly to remove the belongings she'd left before Christmas. He had no idea where she was living. He rebuffed the advice of his mother, sister and friends to seek Maria out.

"If she want to go, I must let her go."

Sometimes a cop had to go with his gut feelings. The husband, especially an estranged husband, was the first suspect in a case like this. Dugas was careful not to mention they'd found a hand that was most likely Maria's, even when he showed the thin wedding band the coroner had removed from the hand.

Alcamo nodded, confirming it was Maria's wedding band, pointing to a slight bulge on one side where the band had worn down unevenly. Dugas told him the band would be returned to him once the case was resolved. Naturally, once Dugas was finished his initial questioning, Alcamo wanted to know what happened to Maria.

"We don't know exactly what happened," said Dugas explaining about the trunk with some of her clothes in it. He watched closely when he told Alcamo about the hand.

The big baker's face seemed frozen for a long minute before he focused newly shocked eyes at Dugas and said, "Oh, my

God. Poor Maria." He made the sign of the cross and wiped a single tear that rolled down his face.

Alcamo did not recognize the trunk, which Dugas had examined closely, finding no markings or anything to indicate ownership. It didn't appear new. "I never seen this trunk before," said Alcamo, but he recognized all of the remaining clothes and shoes as his wife's.

Stepping out of the interview room, Dugas led Alcamo to his desk at the rear of the Bureau and had the big man sit in the wooden chair next to the worn wooden desk as Dugas put the finishing touches to the man's official statement.

"Read this over and sign at the bottom of each page."

As Alcamo read his three page statement, Dugas spotted the acting-commander of the Detective Bureau crossing the squad room with another detective. Lieutenant Ed O'Meara was forty-six, portly, standing five-six with red hair, a moustache and mutton chops along the sides of his wide face. His companion, named McCandless, also stood five-six with dark brown hair, a full moustache and was even thinner than Dugas and a couple years older.

"And who's this?" O'Meara pointed at Alcamo as he arrived. "This the husband?"

Dugas nodded.

"You a Wop?"

Alcamo nodded as Dugas passed him his fountain pen to sign the statement.

"A Moustache Pete sittin' right here," O'Meara turned to McCandless.

"He's not a Moustache Pete," Dugas said, nodding to Alcamo to keep signing. "He doesn't have a moustache, doesn't live in the Quarter, isn't a gangster. He owns his own business."

"The Quarter? You mean Little Palermo? He's Sicilian, ain't he?"

Alcamo nodded again as he signed the last page of his statement.

"There you go," O'Meara waved a hand. "Moustache Pete." He looked at McCandless for support and got nothing. Dugas was surprised when McCandless sided with him. "If he ain't got a handlebar moustache, doesn't stand around leaning on lamp posts in the French Quarter eyeballing passersby, isn't an olive-skinned gangster, then he's just a plain Guinea."

O'Meara glared at McCandless, then turned his glare to Dugas. "What kinda business?"

"Bakery on Esplanade Avenue."

"Pane Fresco?" McCandless now.

"Si," Alcamo answered.

"I've been there. It's a good bakery, lieutenant. A very good one."

"What the hell do you know?" O'Meara grabbed Alcamo's left elbow and pulled the big man up. "I'm gonna sweat this Wop."

"I already did," Dugas said, his voice rising slightly as he pushed back his chair.

"I don't see no marks on him."

Dugas kept his voice firm and low, "We sweat them differently." He stood and leaned his hands on his desk. "You're not taking him. This is my case, lieutenant."

O'Meara was so surprised he let go of Alcamo's elbow, took a menacing step forward and growled, "I out rank you."

"I'm the case officer. You want us to take it up with the superintendent, then let's go. I think the Italian legation is still in town."

That caused O'Meara to pause. The feud between the Irish and Italians, which erupted last October when New Orleans's first police chief David Hennessey was gunned down. The situation exploded when the Sicilians accused of his murder were acquitted only to be lynched in the courtyard of parish prison by an angry mob before they could be released. Word on the street was some of the men lynched were, in fact, innocent. The Italian Government was still threatening war.

"Yeah," McCandless injected. "I heard that the U.S. might have to pay reparations."

O'Meara was dumb, but not that dumb. All they needed was another lynched Italian business man. He huffed at Dugas and tried another tack. "Me friend Donahoe tells me you were cuddling with a darkie what found this trunk."

"I've never cuddled with a man in my life. Sounds like something you Irish do."

This caused O'Meara's eyes to bulge and drew a grin from McCandless.

"Damn Creole," O'Meara stammered. "I ought to thrash you. You don't know how to treat Wops or darkies."

Actually Creoles knew exactly how. Not much trouble between the French and Spanish Creoles and the free-men-of-color until the Kaintocks, as the first Americans were called, came down the Mississippi from Kentucky and points beyond.

"No need to get worked up, lieutenant," Dugas said. "My victim is Sicilian after all."

It wasn't much, but O'Meara took it as a face-saving gesture, stomping off with, "Yeah. Nothin' but a dead Wop."

Alessio Alcamo let out a long breath as the angry lieutenant retreated. Dugas just shrugged as McCandless said, "He's afraid of Captain Gray. Everyone knows you're Gray's fair-haired boy. Calls you 'the smart one'." Gray, their no-nonsense captain, was Irish of course and sharp as a fencer's coil. Everyone, including O'Meara was aware his command was tenuous as well as temporary.

We'll see how smart I am with this case, thought Dugas as he began to lead Alcamo out. Turning, he called back to Mac, "Didn't mean to offend you with that Irish crack."

"You ain't all that smart after all, Mr. French Detective. McCandless is Scottish."

Tuesday, 16 June 1891

Early morning fog covered Bayou St. John completely, extending into the oaks of City Park. The squawk of blue jays and the lilting calls of mockingbirds echoed as Dugas walked up Bayou

Road toward a group of shacks across the bayou from the park.
His ankle was so tight he had trouble moving it and couldn't put
his full weight on it.

He wore black boots today with his gray suit. A fire in a
barrel in front of one shack drew Dugas who watched two men
with tin cups in hand as they moved cautiously away from him.
He was about to call out to them when a voice called out behind
him.

"Mr. Detective Dugas!"

He turned to see Homer Jones come out of a particularly
thick fog bank with another man. Homer smiled, "This here's
John Racey," nodding to his companion. Each carried a tin cup
and Dugas smelled coffee.

Stepping up, Homer added, "He seen something yesterday
morning."

Racey was white, around fifty, about five-five and skinny
with a mop of dirty brown hair on his head, a beard and wore
several layers of clothing. Looking down at his raggedy boots,
Racey said, "I seen a wagon stop right where Homer found the
trunk. Early morning yesterday." He looked up with bloodshot,
drinker's eyes. "A man with blond hair was drivin' the wagon and
I seen him climb down but I didn't see no trunk. Then he drove off
in a hurry."

"Was he alone?"

"Yeah. It was a flatbed wagon with one seat, drawn by a
mule."

"Could you identify the man if you saw him again?"

Racey shook his head. "I hid behind some bushes sos he
won't bother me and seen him turn the wagon around drive away
back up the road."

"Back toward Esplanade?"

"Yes, suh."

"Did he throw anything into the bayou?"

"No. I woulda heard a splash. He didn't go near the
water."

Dugas turned to Homer who said he'd asked everyone he knew and Racey was the only one who saw anything. He showed them Maria's portrait and Homer was quite shaken.

"It was *her* hand?"

"We think so."

Homer shook his head and looked over at the park. "Such a pretty lady."

"You did well," Dugas said as he passed each man a dollar. "Mind if we ask around some more?"

"No, suh. Let's go talk."

They spoke with eleven other men along Bayou Road as the sun rose higher in the sky and the oaks across the bayou came out of the fog with their gray Spanish moss beards, like hulking ghosts, until the sunlight turned their dark leaves into sparkles of green.

None of the other men had seen anything. Dugas thanked Homer again as he walked back down Bayou Road toward Esplanade Avenue. Looking at the sluggish brown bayou, Dugas smelled the brackish water and remembered how this entire area was once a lawless swamp inhabited by thieves and desperate women who did anything to survive. He wondered where they'd gone, then figured their lifespan wasn't that long.

#

Dugas found Donahoe swinging his billy club as he strolled past Smith's Saloon just down Esplanade from the bayou.

"Boyo!" Donahoe called out. "Why you limping? One of them bums bit you on the leg?"

Dugas fought his anger, gritted his teeth instead and said, "Buy you a beer?"

"Is the Pope Catholic?" Donahoe wheeled and led the way into the saloon that smelled of cigar smoke and stale beer. Besides the bartender there were six men at three different tables. Donahoe sidled up to the bar, laid his billy atop and called out, "Barman, two mugs of your best brew."

"Make one a coffee," Dugas said, which drew the attention of two of the men who gave him a long look. Showing Maria's picture to Donahoe, Dugas explained who she was and about Pane Fresco just down the avenue.

"Don't know how I missed a looker like that," Donahoe said shaking his head before downing half his mug in one swallow. The coffee was surprisingly good.

Dugas said, "A blond haired man riding a mule-drawn flat wagon stopped where the trunk was found early yesterday morning only a short time before Homer Jones came across the trunk. He may be our man."

Donahoe pulled the mug from his mouth, his brow furrowed now. "You don't say?" He took a small sip and looked at Dugas differently. "That's good work. I mean there's lotsa blond haired men, but we got somethin' to work with, don't we? And you identified her just from her hand. Maybe youse as smart as they say."

Finishing his beer the burly patrolman took Maria's picture to every table in the bar, had the two men with their hats on remove them, then asked if anyone knew her or a blond man who would have driven a mule-drawn wagon along Bayou Road yesterday morning. No one had.

Stepping back into the sunshine, Donahoe put his bowler back on his head and asked Dugas why he never wore a hat.

"Messes up my hair," Dugas said with a smirk.

Donahoe slapped him on the back. "You're all right, for a Frenchie." He looked down the avenue and said, "How's about I take this side of Esplanade?"

"I'll take the other side."

They met three blocks later outside another saloon. Neither had come up with anything useful. Dugas had made a cursory stop at Pane Fresco and found Alessio Alcamo behind the counter, the man more in a daze than yesterday.

After Dugas bought him another beer, Donahoe assured him he would continue asking about the blond man. "I'll see if I can top what you done." Donahoe grinned and strolled away, swinging his billy.

Dugas went back up Esplanade, crossed the Bayou St. John bridge to the park and asked four couples about the blond man and showed them Maria's picture before exiting the park through the new Alexander Street gate. He looked up at the black wrought-iron gate as he passed through it, at the curved, white wrought-iron letters above announcing: New Orleans City Park.

Dugas limped across the road to a long, two-story wooden building with a pitched roof at the confluence of three thoroughfares – Metairie Road, Alexander and Dumaine Streets. On the second story balcony, which wrapped around the corner of the building, Dugas spotted several couples dining. He felt his stomach rumble as he looked up at the sign out front: Jean Marie Saux's Coffeehouse.

Stepping inside, Dugas was assailed by wonderful cooking scents and was led to a small table against a window along the Metairie Road side of the restaurant. His ankle hurt even more now. He was brought a cup of strong coffee-and-chicory immediately by a mousey, brown haired waitress who handed him a menu

Dugas asked. "What's your name?"

"Alice, sir."

"I've heard the sandwiches here are particularly good."

Alice looked away from Dugas's eyes and nodded. He closed the menu and asked, "Which is the best?"

"Fried oyster sandwich. Best in town."

"Good, I'll have one."

It came quickly. He waited until Alice returned to re-fill his water, as he was half finished the sandwich, to ask about blond haired customers.

"I don't understand, sir."

"Is the manager available?"

"The owner is." Alice hurried off.

Jean Marie Saux was a full-figured woman with long brassy red tresses piled high on her head. Dugas stood as she arrived. She was around forty, trying her best to look younger with plenty of make-up on her face. She was an attractive woman with a soothing voice and wore a snug-fitting dark green dress. When Dugas showed her his badge, she smiled wickedly and pulled out the chair across from the detective.

She allowed him time to come around and hold the chair for her before sitting. The strong perfume she wore momentarily blotted out the food smells. Alice brought her a coffee and refilled Dugas's cup. He waited until both finished mixing cream and sugar in their coffees before bringing out Maria's photo.

"Yes," said Jean Marie. "She's been here. Quiet a lovely."

Dugas went through the logical series of questions and learned Maria had been in often, usually in the afternoons or early evenings and alone most of the time. When pressed as to when Maria wasn't alone, Jean Marie called Alice over to look at the picture.

"Yes, mum. I've seen her but she come alone."

"Did she ever leave with anyone?" Dugas asked, then mentioned the blond haired man for the first time with Jean Marie at the table. Both women shook their heads, Jean Marie adding, "We have many blond haired male customers."

Then she called over the remaining waitresses, one at a time. The last one, a pretty young woman with reddish brown hair and freckles recognized Maria and when asked about the blond haired man, said, "Funny you asked. One of our regulars hasn't been in today or yesterday. A blond man."

"What man?" asked Jean Marie.

"Why Mr. Vitter. Tall man, always dresses nice, wears the frilly shirts."

Dugas had his note pad and pencil in hand and asked the freckle-faced girl her name.

"Kay Alford, sir."

Dugas stood and pulled a chair out for Kay. "Have a seat."

She waited for Jean Marie's nod of approval before sitting. Dugas sat and said, "Tell me about this Mr. Vitter."

"Bill Vitter, sir. He lives over on Encampment Street. A two story house, white with blue trim, the only house with a fenced yard right off Esplanade."

Jean Marie's eyebrows rose. "And how to you know that?"

Kay blushed, shrugged and looked at Dugas. "What else do you want to know, officer?"

Apparently Bill Vitter had begun frequenting Jean Marie Saux's Coffeehouse about a month earlier, came in every day around noon to stay an hour. Maria came in less frequently and always alone. Kay never saw them together but surmised it could have happened easily. "Mr. Vitter. He's a charmer."

#

It was a long shot, but as soon as Vitter opened his door, Dugas felt all the painful limping was worthwhile.

Bill Vitter stood six-two, weighed a good two-hundred pounds which looked to be solid muscle. Dressed in a dark blue suit and matching tie with a frilly shirt, Vitter had his black derby in hand, a row of suitcases lined behind him in the foyer.

"Where's the hansom?" asked Vitter, looking past Dugas, obviously looking for a cab. When he looked back at Dugas, the detective opened the lapel of his coat. Vitter's blue eyes moved to the badge and he took a hesitant step back, his face suddenly pale.

"Going somewhere, Mr. Vitter?" Dugas took a step inside as Vitter backed away, bumping into the suitcases.

"I'm … going to visit a sick aunt."

"Where?"

Vitter looked behind Dugas again, backed around the suitcase and bolted through the foyer. Dugas limped after him, down a hall, through a formal dining room and into the kitchen, pulling out his revolver as Vitter opened the back door and leaped down the back steps into the yard.

Dugas felt his ankle give out as he hurried down the steps. Falling to his knees in the grass, he watched Vitter put a hand up

on the wooden fence and easily clear it. By the time Dugas
reached the fence Vitter was gone.

Hobbling back to the house, Dugas moved through to the
front porch, then gingerly down to the street, pulling out his police
whistle and blowing it until he spotted a beat cop come around
from Esplanade. He waved the man over and went back into the
house.

Donahoe arrived a few minutes after the first copper and
both cops went looking for Vitter while Dugas searched the house.
At first he couldn't place the smell that permeated the house but
thought it was coppery, like the scent of blood, or maybe it was the
copper pipes. He found no trace of blood in the sink or bathtub. In
the study he discovered check stubs. Vitter worked for a Canal
Street Jewelry Store. No wonder he didn't pry Maria's ring from
her finger. A jeweler would know it wasn't worth much, thin as it
was, and probably easily identified.

Dugas left the suitcases last to be searched and moved to
them as Donahoe returned, wiping his brow with the gray
handkerchief and announcing Vitter had disappeared.

"We'll put out a bulletin for him," said Dugas as he spotted
a small pool of liquid next to thickest suitcase. He opened it and
found Maria's head in a burlap sack.

"My God!" Donahoe moaned, then ran outside to throw up
over the porch rail.

O'Meara and McCandless arrived just before the coroner's
man. Taking charge, as if he knew anything about the case,
O'Meara bossed around the curious patrolmen as they arrived, like
moths drawn to a lamp, even tried bossing around the coroner's
assistant who ignored him. The police photographer arrived and
the coroner's man propped up the head for him to photograph.
Dugas took down the everyone's names for his report before
checking the other suitcase for more body parts. Nothing but
men's clothes. The coroner left with the suitcase containing
Maria's head.

McCandless hustled off to the Central Police Station to
issue the bulletin on Vitter to be distributed to every precinct and

to send telegrams to all surrounded jurisdictions. Dugas made one more careful search before locking up Vitter's house with the keys he found in the front door lock. He watched O'Meara holding a conference with the newspapermen assembled outside Vitter's house as he walked over to Esplanade Avenue and Pane Fresco.

"Dugas," Donahoe called out, jogging to catch up. Huffing as he arrived, hands on knees. "I'd appreciate it ... if you wouldn't tell the fellas ... about me ... throwing up."

"Of course not."

Donahoe put a friendly hand on Dugas's shoulder as he stood up, taking in a deep breath. "Gotta hand it to you. You solved it."

"Hand it to me?"

Donahoe's eyes lit up and he shook his head. "You know what I mean." He patted the detective's shoulder, turned and headed back up the avenue.

Dugas didn't want Alessio to read about it in the papers. Bad enough the poor man would have to go the coroner's office to identify Maria's head.

Wednesday, 17 June 1891

It was McCandless who caught Bill Vitter at the Carrollton Train Station. Vitter, wearing a long coat on a steamy morning, still wore his ruffled shirt and shiny black shoes. He surrendered without resistance.

"Good work." Dugas patted Mac on the back as he led Vitter into the same interview room where he'd interviewed Alcamo.

"What's this all about?" Vitter said as Dugas sat across from him with a tablet of ruled paper and two fountain pens. Vitter was trying the outraged-citizen defense. Dugas began slowly, introducing himself then asking what Vitter had done Sunday, June fourteenth.

Vitter looked at the blank wall and said that was so long ago he didn't remember. The innocent-disinterested defense. Vitter went through several defensive positions even going so far as to say, "Maria who?"

Dugas fought hard not to reach over and strangle the bastard and had to steel himself to being friendly with his monstrous murderer.

"Don't sit there and tell me you don't know anything about this."

Vitter looked at the other wall.

"I find you standing next to a suitcase with a woman's head in it and you say, 'Maria who?'." Dugas stood up, acting impatient now. "If you don't want to tell your side of the story, that's your choice. I know what you did. You want to give a statement so the jury will hear your side of the story, I'm here to take it down. If not, we'll go right over to parish prison."

Dugas leaned on the table with both hands. "You don't have to testify at your trial, you know that. This might be the only time the jury will hear your words."

Vitter finally looked at Dugas and said, "It was an accident."

A confession was worth the heartache, worth the pain in Dugas's chest as he wormed the story from Vitter. Dugas put Maria's ring and portrait on the table as Vitter told his story. The killer wouldn't look at them at first. By the end of his tale, Vitter was holding the ring and staring at the photo, tears in his eyes.

And who said alligators couldn't cry? Or was it crocodile tears?

Bill Vitter had seen Maria Alcamo at Jean Marie Saux's Coffeehouse on several occasions. She was always alone and didn't meet his eye as most other women who were alone did. Eventually she met his eye, Saturday evening, and when she left he followed her across to the park. Beneath the Alexander gate, he greeted her, tipping his hat and asked if he could walk with her through the park. She went willingly to his house and spent the weekend with him. Sunday evening, she turned on him, becoming abusive, demanding money.

"She struck me and I struck her back and she fell and didn't get up." Vitter stared at the portrait as he softly spoke, "It was an accident."

Dugas kept his face expressionless, hoping Vitter couldn't hear the stammer of his heart, see the loathing in his eyes.

"Then what did you do?"

"I had no choice. I had to get rid … I had to get her out of my house."

Dugas copied the words verbatim.

"So what did you do?"

"I took her apart."

Jesus, such a nice phrase for dismembering someone.

"What did you do with the pieces?"

Vitter swallowed and said he put the pieces in a trunk and took the trunk to the lake, using his neighbor's wagon, and threw the trunk into the water.

"What about Maria's head?"

Vitter blinked at him and said nothing.

"Were you keeping it as a souvenir?"

Vitter looked away again and Dugas knew he'd hit home. He went on to ask where Vitter was going when he came to the door. The sick aunt story again. Dugas tried to get details but the man was vague as to his aunt's name, saying she lived in small town in Mississippi. He couldn't recall the name of the town either.

"How would you get there without knowing the name?"

Vitter picked up Maria's ring and stared at it. Dugas wrote 'no response' next to that question on the statement.

"What about the second trunk, the portmanteau with the clothes in it?"

Vitter nodded. "I forgot to throw her clothes away so I put them in an old portmanteau and tried to throw it in Bayou St. John only some men were there, so I just dropped it."

"Why did you put the hand in the portmanteau?"

"Hand?" He could see Vitter was confused.

"Her left hand," Dugas said. "Where do you think I found the ring?"

Vitter sat frozen, staring at Dugas, the man having no idea how Maria's hand had fallen in the portmanteau as he was getting rid of her clothes. Vitter closed his eyes. Dugas kept his open but could see, in his mind's eye, Vitter frantically cleaning up the blood, tossing body parts into the trunk, tossing clothes into the portmanteau, Maria's hand falling in with the clothes that bore her laundry mark.

"It was an accident," Vitter concluded as he signed his statement.

Accident? Wait until the jury sees the photos of Maria's head.

Dugas watched him sign each page, knowing it would hang him. Watching the man's neck snap would be Dugas's only relief from the pain in his chest.

He looked again at Maria's portrait, at the mischievous glint in her dark eyes and felt sick. It wasn't enough to just catch her killer. As he stood up, he was glad he'd left his revolver out in his desk. Maria seemed to look back at him and he felt a heartache. Maria Alcamo was twenty years old.

Thursday, 18 June 1891

McCandless came up to Dugas's desk with a note in flowing script.

"Just came by post. It's perfumed," he said, handing Dugas the note, moving around so he could read it too. Dugas opened it and both read:

Dear Detective Dugas,

Hope you won't think me as too forward but I haven't been able to stop thinking about your dark brown eyes.

You know where to find me,

Kay

Alford

McCandless slapped Dugas's shoulder. "You hound!"

Dugas tried to compose himself as McCandless walked away, calling over his shoulder, "Better watch yourself with a woman named Alford. That's a Scottish name."

The Gold Bug of Jean Lafitte

"It is the loveliest thing in creation!"
from *The Gold Bug* by Edgar Allan Poe

Monday, 13 July 1891, early afternoon
The Creole townhouse at 77 Toulouse Street stood out from the other townhouses lining the narrow French Quarter Street because of the small crowd gathered across the street and the police officer standing outside its worn, cypress door. Dugas approached from Chartres Street and the police officer took off his powder-blue bowler hat, wiped his brow with a handkerchief and said, "Good afternoon, Detective Dugas."

"Good afternoon, Officer Clavin."

Clavin ran the handkerchief through his short reddish-brown hair before returning the bowler to his head.

"Figured they'd be calling you," he told Dugas as the detective stepped up. "All these people speak French."

Dugas pulled his note pad and a pencil from his coat pocket and jotted a brief description of the building — three stories with a black wrought-iron balcony running along the second floor — the building's stucco facade painted a drab yellow.

Detective Jacques Dugas was a lean man, six feet tall, with an olive complexion, a thick moustache and Mediterranean dark brown eyes. His gray suit was light-weight and his dress shirt collar un-starched to combat the heat and humidity of another fierce New Orleans summer. At twenty-six years old, Dugas was the youngest detective on the force.

"They're in apartment 3D," Clavin advised, pointing to a white sign with maroon letters next to the door. The sign read: *E. Legrand, Professor of Magnetic Physiology.*

"They?"

"Two bodies. A man and a girl." Clavin looked away nervously. "'Ere comes Doctor Miller now."

A portly man carrying a black case rushed around the corner from Decatur Street. Holding on to his brown derby, the doctor shuffled toward them.

Dugas turned back to the building and asked Clavin. "Whom did you mean when you said, 'They all speak French'?"

"The landlord and the other tenants."

"Ah."

Dugas ascended the narrow stairs to the third floor. The building smelled of stale beer and dust. Apartment 3D was at the rear of the building, its door slightly ajar. Dugas pushed open the door but remained in the doorway, letting his eyes adjust to the dimness inside.

The shutters were drawn and the only illumination came from two candles at either end of the small apartment. Flickering candlelight danced off the walls and cast black shadows across the room. It took Dugas a moment to realize the floor was littered with stacks of yellowed newspapers, magazines and piles of books. He immediately smelled the unmistakable odor of chloroform.

Footsteps arrived on the landing behind Dugas who leaned out of the way to allow the doctor entrance. Dr. Miller stepped into the room, nodding as he passed and flipped on the electric light switch just inside the door. A huge crystal and brass chandelier, hanging from the center of the water-stained ceiling, bathed the room in bright light. The doctor and Dugas blinked.

"Damn," the doctor said to the brightness. He let out a nasally breath and began weaving his way through the stacks of books.

Dugas stepped in and saw them on the bed. Both lay on their backs, the man nearest them. Wearing a white shirt and dark pants with suspenders, the man was barefoot, his right leg dangling from the bed. The woman was naked, her head turned toward the man, her long brown hair covering her face. Her skin was chalky white beneath the electric light.

Dugas followed the doctor who, upon arriving at the far side of the bed, reached for the woman's hand. She was young. Twenty maybe. The man appeared closer to forty and his chest was covered in blood. Dugas wiped perspiration from his temples and picked up another scent, faintly. Roses.

"Still warm," the doctor said as he let the woman's hand down and pulled a stethoscope from his bag. He pressed it against the woman's chest, moved it twice, then let out a long breath and belched.

"Dead."

The doctor moved around the bed for the man. Dugas stepped out of his way and kicked something that rolled. A blue medicine bottle tumbled across the floor toward the fireplace. Something smoldered in the fireplace, giving off an orange glow.

Dugas retrieved the bottle just as the doctor declared the man was also dead. The bottle reeked of chloroform. The word printed on a red label on the bottle confirmed his suspicion. The label was from J. Broussard, Pharmacist. Dugas had passed Broussard's Pharmacy moments earlier, around the corner on Chartres.

"Aha," Dr. Miller said, then hiccupped. He leaned forward and picked a small knife off the bed next to the man's left hand. He held the knife up for Dugas, then carefully placed it on a stack of books next to the bed.

"Self-inflicted," Dr. Miller declared, waving at the man on the bed. He hiccupped again and said, "Open the windows. The chloroform is sickening."

Dugas moved to the nearest window and pulled it up, unlocked the louvered shutters, and threw the shutters open. He took in a deep breath of warm, summer air and glanced down into the dilapidated courtyard behind the building. A scraping sound caused him to look up in time to see three boys scurry over the roof of the building directly beyond the courtyard.

"Look here," Dr. Miller said. The doctor had pulled the hair away from the woman's face and pointed at her mouth. "Her lips are burned from the chloroform."

Dugas stepped closer and caught a whiff of the doctor's whiskey breath. The woman's full lips were stained purple. He looked at her body again — lovely in its naked beauty. Her legs were long and slim and her toenails painted pink.

Such a tragedy — Dugas could not help from thinking. Such a beautiful girl. Suddenly he felt his neck flush. He wanted to pull the sheet over the body, to cover her, but he knew there was no dignity in death, no privacy for a corpse. Once a young, vibrant woman, she was now a specimen to be examined, probed and studied like an insect beneath a microscope. He looked away.

Dr. Miller sat on a stack of books a few feet from the bed, and pulled a note pad from his black case. Dugas looked around. On a small wooden table next to the bed lay a stack of pink cards and two sheets of paper. The sheets were pharmacist's receipts, both from J. Broussard Pharmacy and both in the name of Dr. E. Legrand. Dugas noted the date on both receipts were today's date.

He picked up one of the pink cards, which appeared to be a business card. In neat calligraphy, the card read:

Let us look for truth.

Let us do good.

Let us be magnetized!

Dr. Etienne Legrand

77 Rue Toulouse

New Orleans

"Magnetized?" Dugas said.

"What?" Dr. Miller hiccupped just as a man sporting a red handle-bar moustache and mutton chops stepped into the room. Detective Patrick Shannon waved at Dugas, pulled off his tan derby and introduced himself to Dr. Miller. Although he stood the same height as Dugas, Shannon was bulkier and appeared larger in his pin-striped brown suit, two sizes too small for him.

Dr. Miller asked, "What did you say about 'Magnetized'?"

The man on the bed suddenly *sat up*. Dr. Miller fell off the stack of books. The man on the bed turned, looked down at the dead woman and started crying.

"Mon Dieu! Mon Dieu!" The man pulled at his hair and cried out in French, "I meant to die. I meant to die!"

Dugas quickly jotted what the man said in his notes. He could see Shannon moving forward, past the doctor who was struggling to rise.

The man on the bed started searching the bed and cried out. "Where is it? Where?"

Seeing the knife on the nearby stack of books, he reached for it only to have Shannon grab his hand.

"We'll 'ave none 'o that!"

The man pulled back and cringed away from Shannon. He seemed to notice the doctor for the first time, then Dugas.

"Are you Dr. Legrand?" Dugas asked.

The man nodded, opened his mouth for a faint, "Oui." Then the man swooned and fell off the bed.

"Dammit to hell," Shannon growled as he reached for the man.

The doctor managed to get up, hiccupping as he examined his stethoscope. Dugas went to the bed and took the woman's wrist. Cool to his touch, he felt for a pulse but there was none. He felt for her carotid artery and her neck was cool. He pulled up her eyelid and her eye and face had the unmistakable, unfocused look of death.

Dr. Miller stepped over and handed Dugas the stethoscope, belching again and teetering as he stood. Dugas checked the body. No pulse. He pressed the stethoscope against his own chest and heard his heartbeat plainly.

"I'll attend to him," Dr. Miller told Shannon. "You go down and tell that copper to fetch an ambulance."

The doctor sat Legrand up and administered to him. Dugas resumed searching the apartment, making note of the chifforobe in the corner with several men's suits inside and a pink dress on a wooden hanger. On the mantle above the fireplace stood twelve magnets of different sizes. They were lined in a row and spaced equally apart. They appeared to be the only objects in the place that were not thrown about.

Loud voices boomed outside the door. Dugas moved that way as Clavin backed into the room. A red-faced man tried to push his way past Clavin.

"Hold on," Clavin ordered, shoving the man back.

The man stopped and stared past Clavin at the bed for a moment before collapsing against the door frame.

"Julie! My Julie!" The man wailed and then lunged past Clavin.

Dugas caught him between two stacks of magazines and with Clavin's help, moved the man back into the hallway.

"Oh no. No. No!" The man fell to the floor and covered his head with his hands.

Dugas put a friendly hand on Clavin's shoulder and asked him go back down and keep anyone else from entering the building.

"And keep those who are inside – inside."

Clavin took off his bowler. "This man says the woman is his daughter."

Dugas urged Clavin back down the stairs and let the crying man — cry. Dr. Miller covered the woman's body with a sheet.

Presently, Shannon returned with two white-clad ambulance attendants carrying a gurney. Dugas helped the crying man out of the way, standing him in the corner of the hall next to the hall's lone window. He opened the window and shutters and waited.

Obviously a carpenter, the man wore a leather apron with a hammer dangling from a loop and several pockets stuffed with other tools. His soiled shirt was worn badly near the collar and his work pants had small holes at the knees. The man finally quit wailing, as the gurney with Legrand exited the room, followed by Shannon. The man asked, "Is Dr. Legrand dead?"

Dugas shook his head and asked, "What is your name, monsieur?"

"Louis. Louis Maigret." The man's callused hands wiped tears from his eyes. He looked into Dugas's eyes. "What happened?" He looked toward the body on the bed again and sank to the floor with his back against the wall.

Going down on his haunches next to the man Dugas said, "Tell me, monsieur. Tell me what you know."

The man spoke quickly and Dugas hurried to write every word in his notes.

Louis Maigret met Dr. Legrand near Jackson Square about a year ago. Legrand was passing out business cards. Newly arrived from Paris, Legrand seemed a refined gentleman and Maigret was honored when Legrand struck up a friendship with a common carpenter.

Using *magnetism*, Dr. Legrand was able to cure many maladies, especially in women and his practice grew steadily. Julie had no malady but spent a great deal of time with the good doctor. She was a medium for Legrand as they searched for the treasure of Jean Lafitte.

"I'm sorry," Dugas interrupted. "Did you say treasure?"

"Dr. Legrand was privileged to information that Jean Lafitte buried a great treasure in the swamps and islands of Barataria. He needed a medium, a young girl, a *virgin* to help him."

Dugas tried to keep his face as expressionless as possible as he asked, "How?"

Maigret described Legrand's *treatments* in detail. Dugas jotted feverishly.

"I witnessed the first sessions."

Legrand explained how Legrand, using hypnosis, aided by chloroform, would put Julie into a trance where she was more easily drawn to his magnetic powers. Magnets were placed on Julie as she lay on the bed. Legrand would sometimes rub the magnets on her and she would talk, often in foreign tongues. She gave directions to the treasure.

"She knew no language except English. I would not even speak French to her because English is the language we need to succeed in America, yet she spoke in tongues. Not gibberish, 'cause I understood some of the words. Spanish. Italian. Latin.

"They went several times down to Barataria and Grand Isle." The man covered his face with his hands again and wept.

Dugas waited, wiping perspiration from his face with his handkerchief. Dr. Miller peeked out of the room but ducked back in quickly. A mockingbird landed on the window sill, bounced once, then flew off. Maigret's crying finally subsided.

"Julie —" the man's voice cracked. He sucked in a deep breath. "My daughter — a strong-willed girl. I was afraid. You see, she hung around with all sorts of boys and I thought she'd be safe with Dr. Legrand."

Tears streamed again down the man's face.

A sourness in Dugas's stomach, from not eating lunch, seemed to acidify as he stood up and waited next to the grieving father. Footsteps echoed up the stairs and presently two white-clad mortuary attendants appeared, carrying another gurney. Their dark brown faces glistened with sweat.

A few minutes later, Dr. Miller led the gurney out, a white sheet covering the corpse of Julie Maigret. The father watched silently, blinking tears from his eyes. Dugas pulled Shannon aside and asked him to continue searching the room. "I will finish interviewing the father and the landlord and tenants."

Taking off his derby, Shannon nodded and returned to the death room.

Dugas turned back to the father, who was now standing and said, "Today, monsieur. Tell me how Julie's day started and how she came to be here *today*."

Monday, 13 July 1891, late afternoon

Dugas tucked his note pad and pencil back into his coat pocket as he stepped out of Broussard's Pharmacy, passing several Moustache-Petes — olive-skinned Sicilians with long black moustaches who always wore black suits. He looked them in the eye, but didn't stare. The Italians, who had been talking, stopped talking until Dugas passed.

Ever since the murder of Chief of Police David Hennessey, the previous year, and the subsequent lynching of the Italians at Parish Prison by an angry mob, a shaky truce existed between the police and the large Sicilian population, centered mostly in the old French Quarter. There were threats and vandalisms but not even the most brazen Mafiosi would attack a policemen.

Dugas walked to the corner of Toulouse Street and looked toward the yellow facade of number 77. A small crowd still stood across the street, but Clavin was gone. He went back to the house and found Shannon sitting on the steps just inside the doorway.

"I found these." Shannon held up a leather notebook. "I think it's Legrand's notes of his experiments. They're in French."

Dugas took the notebook and opened it. In neat copperplate printing, as if done by a press, yet written in pen and ink, was the title in French: *Experiments in Magnetism by Doctor Etienne Legrand at New Orleans, Louisiana, in the United States of America in the year of our Lord 1891.*

The rest of the notebook was in French all right, but gibberish. Numbers listed out of order, words rammed together that had no meaning. It wasn't even a code. It was — insane.

"What does it say?" Shannon asked.

Dugas interpreted one passage verbatim — 'a fox and a boat and the sun at night and the chirp of the marsh comes running into a glen green and organ and purple and liver paste a goose.' He flipped a page and read — 'revolution and brick courtyard, barnyard, yardstick, drumstick, broken stick, lance, upside down, falls of water'.

Shannon's brow was furrowed. "The man's a lunatic."

"Quite possibly." Dugas tucked both notebooks under his arm as Shannon stood up and dusted his pants.

"There are more books up there. All in French 'o course. Some look scientific. Some are novels."

The two policemen stepped outside and the people across the narrow street separated and left the area.

"Novels?"

"I recognized the names," said Shannon as he opened his small notebook and read, "Balzac. Flaubert. Victor Hugo. Even uneducated Irishmen like me know those are French writers. Am I right?"

"You are correct."

Shannon flipped the page in his notebook. "There was one in English. *Tales of the Grotesque and Arab* — something, by Edgar Allan Poe."

"Arabesque."

Shannon closed his notebook. "I read a Poe story once. Something about a black cat."

"It's called 'The Black Cat'."

"You don't say." Shannon led the two up Toulouse. "I've worked meself up a healthy thirst, monsieur. Join me for a brew."

Dugas nodded and walked alongside his partner away from the death house. As they went up the narrow street, he could not help but thinking how misery was a frequent visitor to this particular street. In 1788, the great fire, which destroyed nearly eighty percent of New Orleans, had begun on Toulouse Street. Apropos for a street named for a bastard son of Louis XIV.

The sharp scent of tomato gravy wafting from a nearby house caused Dugas's stomach to grumble. He'd rather a meal than a beer, but knew there was no talking Shannon out of going to his favorite bar.

The old Quarter, an ever-growing Italian slum, was a shadow of its former glory. Littered with rickety vegetable carts, sheets hanging from lace balconies, its Creole cottages crumbling in disrepair, its alleys filled with refuse. Several dark haired boys raced past Dugas, yelling at each other in Italian as they played.

They caught a mule-driven streetcar up to Basin Street, both discreetly showing their badges to the driver. Policemen, as well as priests and nuns, rode free. They caught another up to Iberville Street to Tom Anderson's saloon. Settling at the bar, while Patrick Shannon downed his first beer, Dugas had the barman prepare an egg sandwich for him as he jotted questions in his notebook, questions he'd ask of the charlatan who called himself *Dr.* Etienne Legrand.

Monday, 13 July 1891, early evening

Legrand lay in a private room along the backside of Charity Hospital. An N.O.P.D. man sat on a folding chair in the hall.

"No visitors," the bored copper told Dugas as the detective stepped up.

Dugas opened his jacket to show his gold star-and-crescent N.O.P.D. badge pinned inside his lapel. "I am Detective Jacques Dugas."

When he entered the patient's room, Legrand sat up immediately. He wore a white nightshirt.

"I protest!" Legrand shrieked in French.

"Shut up." Dugas closed the door. He had planned to go easy, to be nice, to get Legrand to talk by stealth, but seeing the smug look on Legrand's face as he lay in a private room, Dugas changed his mind instantly.

"I protest!" Legrand shouted again.

"We speak in English, you two-bit charlatan." Dugas moved to the bed, grabbed Legrand by the throat and squeezed hard. Legrand flailed his arms and gasped.

Dugas waited several seconds before letting go. Legrand sank back on the bed and gasped to catch his breath. Dugas pulled his note pad from his pocket, thumbed back through his notes until he reached the proper page.

"When you said, 'I meant to die' — did you mean it?"

Legrand rubbed his throat.

Dugas withdrew his snub-nosed. .38 caliber Smith & Wesson, cocked the hammer and pressed it against Legrand's left temple. "Now if you put your finger here." Dugas grabbed Legrand's hand and pulled it up to the gun. "Put it right here against the trigger and pull — you won't ever have to say you meant to die again."

Legrand's mud-brown eyes were ovaled, his lower lip quivering.

"Do you want me to do it for you?"

Tears formed in Legrand's eyes as he shook his head slowly.

"Then we'll have no more protesting, now will we?"

Dugas uncocked the revolver and slipped it back into its holster on his right hip. Flipping through his notes, Dugas said, "When did you decide to kill her? This morning? Yesterday?"

Legrand blinked wildly at Dugas.

"At nine a.m. you bought a bottle of chloroform at Broussard's Pharmacy. At noon you came rushing back in a frenzy, even angry, and purchased another bottle." Dugas skipped over Broussard's description of Legrand as a 'gentleman' and 'scientist'. "The first bottle wasn't enough, was it?"

Dugas looked up from his notes at the muddy eyes. Legrand blinked again. Dugas reached and tapped the stock of his thirty-eight.

Legrand waved his arms again and said, "This is a plot, monsieur. A plot to besmirch the fair name of France."

Dugas almost laughed.

"You, monsieur. You are hounding me because I am French. I demand to see the Counsel!"

Dugas pressed his knees against and bed and leaned forward, causing Legrand to lean away.

"I am French, you ass."

"You are American-French. I am French!"

"What you are, monsieur, is a murderer. And I am the man who will take you to the gallows."

Legrand became still. Dugas leaned away and flipped through his notes again. "Now, Julie Maigret has been *assisting* you for six months. Because she is a virgin, correct?"

Legrand closed his eyes. The opened them and suddenly yanked off the sheet covering his legs. He jumped out of the other side of the bed, leaped to the window and climbed up on the window sill. Reaching for the heating pipes overhead, Legrand pulled himself up, kicking his feet against the wall.

The door opened and the copper stuck his head in.

"What the hell's he doing?"

"I have no idea," Dugas said as Legrand shimmied higher up the pipe.

A doctor appeared behind the copper and said, "What is the meaning of this?"

Legrand howled like a wolf, craned his neck forward and fell head first to the floor. The doctor rushed to his aid as a nurse hurried in, pushing Dugas aside. Legrand moaned loudly as the doctor checked his head. Dugas put his note pad back into the coat pocket and headed for the door.

"Wait!" The doctor pointed to Dugas. "Who are you to question my patient?"

Still moving, Dugas turned and said, "I am the man who will make certain that charlatan dies."

"Mon Dieu!" Legrand cried. "Mon Dieu!"

Wednesday, 15 July 1891, late morning

Standing between two cement sepulchres near the rear of St. Louis Cemetery No. 2, Dugas and Shannon watched at a discreet distance as Julie Maigret's casket was slid into a oven tomb in the back wall of the cemetery. Wearing another light-weight suit, his blue one, Dugas felt perspiration under his arms and along the small of his back. The unrelenting, semi-tropical sun beat down on his exposed head. Humidity, like a bowl of steaming rice, sweltered around them.

Shannon fanned himself with his black derby. He wore a black pin-striped suit today. Fifty yards away, Louis Maigret wore his only suit, also black. A priest said a prayer and sprinkled holy water into the oven tomb. Dugas counted the people in attendance. Eighteen.

"I heard the wounds on his chest barely broke the skin," Shannon said.

Dugas nodded.

"What about his head, when he dove?"

"Headache."

"I was thinking," Shannon said, "Maybe we should contact the French police about this character."

Dugas smiled to himself. "I telegraphed the Sûreté yesterday.

Shannon fanned his coat. "Good. Good. I wonder why Dr. Miller thought he was dead."

"Combination of chloroform and whiskey."

"What?"

"Legrand's chloroform and Miller's whiskey."

Dugas noticed a veiled woman in black move to Louis Maigret and wrap her arms around him. The small crowd began to filter back through the cemetery, led by the priest. Two impatient gravediggers peeked out from behind another sepulchre, obviously waiting for Maigret and the woman to leave so they could quickly plaster over the oven tomb, sealing the casket in the long wall of tombs.

"What did the autopsy reveal?" Shannon asked. "She die of chloroform poisoning?"

"Yes. It also revealed a motive."

"Yes?" Shannon bounced on his toes.

"Legrand needed a virgin for his experiments, correct?"

"If you say so." Shannon fanned himself faster with his hat.

"Julie Maigret was with child."

"Damn!"

Standing away from the woman in black, Maigret reached up and touched the casket before leading the woman back through the cemetery. As they passed Dugas and Shannon, Maigret looked their way and told the woman something. The woman pulled away from him and hurried toward the detectives. Dugas stepped forward to meet her. When she lifted the veil from her face and focused her large blue eyes at Dugas, he felt a sudden surge in his heartbeat.

"Monsieur detective," she said with a deep, breathless voice. "I am Julie's sister and I must speak with you." Beautiful. There was no other way to describe her. Her wide eyes and small nose, the line of her cheeks, round chin combined to make her even prettier than her sister. This slightly older version of Julie wore her dark brown hair in long waves.

She raised a shaking left hand to her full lips. "Monsieur, you must help me."

"Of course," Dugas answered, wanting to reach out to still her shaking hand. He could see Maigret approaching behind the woman.

"Monsieur, have you found the gold bug?"

"The what?"

She leaned closer and Dugas picked up a scent of roses. Maigret arrived and placed a hand on the woman's shoulder.

"Monsieur," her voice rose. "You must find the gold bug! It is in Legrand's room."

"No," Maigret complained. No!"

The woman pulled away, turned and headed quickly for the carriages waiting at the front of the cemetery. Shannon stepped next to his partner and let out a long sigh. Dugas started to follow, but Maigret raised a hand.

"Monsieur detective. My daughter is distraught. Perhaps you can question her later?"

Dugas watched as the woman stepped through the gates of the cemetery and climbed into a dark carriage, a very fine carriage. Looking back at Maigret, Dugas asked, "What is your daughter's name?"

Maigret let out a long breath. "Bridgette. She is my eldest. Twenty-three. Bridgette Madison. She lives on St. Charles with the family of her husband." Maigret choked back a sob. "Bridgette married a rich American last year. He was on the *Utopia*. You remember the collision off Gibraltar? It was in all the papers."

Last March. Dugas remembered. The British ironclad *Anson* collided with the *Utopia*, sending her down with over five hundred souls, including several New Orleanians.

"First her husband and now this." Maigret wiped a tear from his eye. Faintly, he whispered, "Now this."

Wednesday, 15 July 1891, late afternoon

Dugas checked his notes again for the address Maigret had reluctantly given for his daughter, the widow Madison. He stepped off the streetcar on St. Charles at the corner of Marengo. The house was in the center of the block along the river side of the avenue. A sprawling, three story Greek Revival home, painted pale yellow, the wide front yard held two large oaks and an immense magnolia tree.

Dugas moved through a black, wrought iron gate and up the brick walkway. Cooler under the trees, the air smelled of freshly cut grass. He climbed the twenty marble steps to a wide second story gallery with six gilded Corinthian columns and rang the bell next to the cut-glass front door. Expecting a servant to answer, Dugas was surprised when Bridgette opened the door, her eyes ovaled in genuine surprise. She had her hair pinned up in barrettes at the temples. She looked over her shoulder for a moment and Dugas could not help staring at the curve of her bare neck. He remembered her father said she was twenty-three. She grabbed his hand and pulled him into a foyer, past a wide staircase and into a parlor. She closed the door, moved to a small table and turned on an electric lamp.

Bridgette wore a white dress, light-weight, a summer cotton dress (common for New Orleans women during the hottest months), her figure plainly visible with the light behind her. She was taller than her sister — nearly five feet, ten inches.

"Monsieur, we must keep our voices down." Again the breathless voice. "Did you find it?"

Dugas shook his head. "I just came from Legrand's. What does it look like?"

Bridgette moved to the French doors overlooking the front yard. "It is brilliant gold, perhaps three inches in length. A golden bug with six short legs and two stones of polished onyx embedded in it. It will be on a gold chain."

Dugas reached into his coat pocket for a business card to pass to Bridgette. With the sunlight behind her, as she stood in front of the glass doors, Bridgette's body was visible through the diaphanous dress. Dugas tried not to stare but only managed to move his gaze up to Bridgette's gorgeous face as he stepped closer to give her his card.

"I searched the place thoroughly. For nearly three hours."

Bridgette fidgeted with a small pink ribbon on the collar of her dress.

"I found books on magnetism and hypnotism and vampirism and even lycanthropy."

"Lycanthropy?" Bridgette blinked her eyes and seemed to come out of a momentary fog.

"The belief that a human can change into the shape of an animal. Usually a wolf."

"Werewolves. Legrand talked about the Loup Garous in the deep swamps around Barataria. He believed in them." The tone in her voice showed she did not.

Stepping forward, she grabbed Dugas's lapel. "Monsieur. You *must* find it!" Her breath fell across his lips.

Dugas licked his lips and said, "Why?"

Bridgette shot a frightened look toward the parlor door. "It is the most beautiful object in creation. It has *powers*. Do you understand? Ancient powers."

The door suddenly opened and Bridgette jumped away from Dugas, toward the French doors. An elderly woman in a long black dress stepped in and glared at Dugas.

"Mama. This is the police." Bridgette's voice wavered. "He is here about my sister."

The woman's mouth opened into an 'O' and she nodded slowly before backing out of the door. Just before closing it, she gave Bridgette a disapproving look. "Do not stand next to the windows."

Bridgette ignored the remark and let out a long sigh of relief when the door closed.

"Detective Dugas," her voice calmer now. "It is imperative, *most* imperative you find the gold bug. Will you please search again for it. Please?"

The door opened again and the old woman came in, followed by a tall Negro butler carrying a silver tray.

"Tea," the woman announced in a sharp, unfriendly voice.

Bridgette stepped around Dugas and said, "Detective Dugas was just leaving." Reaching back, she touched his hand and held it a moment.

The old woman waved the butler to a small serving table. "Well then we can have our tea right here."

Bridgette's shoulders sank. "I will walk you out," she told Dugas.

"Alvin will see him to the door," the old woman said. The butler hurriedly set up two tea settings and then started for the parlor door.

Dugas stepped around Bridgette.

"You will keep me informed?" Bridgette said behind him.

Dugas turned back for one more look.

"Of course," he said, his heart continued stammering as he followed Alvin through the foyer and then into the bright afternoon sunlight.

Wednesday, 15 July 1891, early evening

Bordered by streets with amiable names like Orleans, Tremé, St. Ann and Marais, the brooding, grim Parish Prison stood like a concrete, medieval monolith a few short blocks from the elegant balconies of the French Quarter. Dugas passed a number of people waiting to visit inmates as he entered the prison. The waiting room smelled of perfume, probably from the inordinate amount of ladies, he figured as he slipped past the visitors into the detention area.

A hulking prison guard with a protruding brow led Dugas through a labyrinth of dark corridors to the second floor where Legrand stood alone in his cell. In a white shirt and gray prison dungarees, a white patch on his head, Legrand moved forward when he saw Dugas and gripped his cell bars.

"I demand to know why I'm being held incommunicado."

The guard slapped Legrand's hands. "Aw, shuddap! Ya damn Frog."

Legrand pulled his hands back and set a pleading stare at Dugas.

"Ya can talk to the bastard through the bars," the guard said and turned to leave.

"Why are my visitors not allowed to see me?" Legrand asked.

"Visitors?" The guard stopped. "All them pathetic women! What are ya, some kinda moor-lock, one 'a them man-witches?" The guard walked away, adding over his shoulder, "Ya ain't getting' near any of them women, ya' degenerate."

Legrand grabbed the bars again and yanked at them. "I demand to communicate with the French Embassy in Washington. When France declares war on this barbaric country, we'll see who laughs last!"

He looked at Dugas who took out his note pad and said, "Tell me, Monsieur Deschamps, how did you come up with the name Legrand?"

The man's eyes widened as he obviously recognized Dugas from the hospital now. He let go of the bars again and shoved his hands in his pockets.

Dugas pulled a yellow telegram from his coat pocket. "According to the Sûreté, you were born Etienne Deschamps in Paris in 1850." Reading from the telegram now, Dugas added, "You were convicted of fraud three times, monsieur." Dugas looked back at the man. "Dabbling in the occult, I am told."

Legrand backed away to the small cot attached to the rear wall and sat.

Dugas waited.

Legrand finally spoke, "I will say nothing of Paris. It is too painful. I miss it too much." He stared hard at Dugas. "Have you ever been to Paris?"

Dugas nodded.

"Bon. You said you were French-American." Legrand looked around his small cell with darting, rat-like eyes. "Hopefully, you are a man of some culture, as limited as it may be in his despicable country."

Dugas waited.

"Do you seriously believe this — this escapade will end in anything but acquittal for me?" Legrand stared at Dugas who kept his face from revealing anything.

"Murder? They have charged me with *murder!*" Legrand buried his face in his hands, almost theatrically. "I may be a charlatan, a fakir. I may have been careless in my administration of chloroform, but I am no *murderer*. Mon Dieu. It is not possible."

Legrand came quickly to the cell bars and added, "Monsieur, Julie Maigret was a whore. I thought she was a virgin, but she was a whore. Do you understand?"

Dugas took out his note pad and wrote exactly what Legrand said about being a charlatan and a fakir and the careless administration of chloroform.

"It was an accident," Legrand went on. "Her death was an accident and I tried to kill myself after. Isn't it obvious, even to you?" When Dugas did not respond, Legrand retreated to his cot and sat on it. After several long minutes, he said, "I am a victim of prejudice because I am a foreigner."

Dugas waited but Legrand seemed finished.

"Monsieur," Dugas finally spoke, "Tell me about the gold bug."

Legrand glared at Dugas, reached for the bars on the far side of his cell and began climbing. When he reached the top, he pulled his legs up, propelled himself out and landed head first on the cement floor and lay motionless.

Dugas walked back to the guard and told him.

"Dammit. He keeps doin' that we gonna haveta chain him to his bed!" The guard snatched up a set of handcuffs and a ring of keys and hurried back to the cell. Dugas followed but remained outside as the guard picked up a groggy Legrand and plopped him on the cot. "Got the hardest goddamn head I ever saw," the guard added as he cuffed Legrand to his bed.

"He got loose yesterday, on his way to the infirmary. Ran down the hall like a lunatic, screaming he was free. Son-of-a-bitch fell down the stairs. Landed on his head. That's how he got the new bandage."

The guard led Dugas out, sneering at several women sitting in the inmate visiting area.

"You seen all them?" The guard spit disgustedly on the cement floor. "They're here to see him."

Maybe, Dugas thought. I'll have a little talk with the ladies.

Wednesday, 15 July 1891, midnight

Dugas knew he was dreaming and wanted the dream to go on —

He and Bridgette walked arm and arm along the banquette in the French Quarter. It was night and she wore a maroon, satin dress, her hair hanging free to her shoulders, her lips a bright, shimmering crimson, those blue eyes bright as they stared into his eyes. She smiled demurely as he put his hand on her waist to guide her into a fine, New Orleans restaurant, one he could never afford on a policeman's salary.

Succulent scents filled the air as they were led by a prim maître'd through the restaurant, people staring at Bridgette as they passed to a small patio out back where they dined under a tin awning. A light rain tapped on the awning as they ate a delicate shrimp soufflé, tangy French onion soup and crisp trout almandine, all washed down by a light, pale French wine. Chocolates came for dessert and a fine brougham drove them to their hotel.

They made love with the balcony doors open to a driving rain that cooled their steaming bodies. It was delicious. It was magnificent. It was a heart pounding affair until Dugas woke with a start. Two cats outside were howling at one another, followed by loud hissing.

He closed his eyes tightly and reached for the dream.

He dreamt again, but not of Bridgette. A swarm of gold bugs came as a dark cloud over the roofs of New Orleans. Their incessant buzz wavered as they flew into open windows, scattering children in playgrounds, running carriages into one another.

Dugas realized they weren't bugs. They were flying spiders, golden spiders from hell with long, hooked talons and poison fangs. As large as a man's hand, the spiders fell on the people of New Orleans and felled them in their wake. Dugas woke again, sat up in bed and rubbed his head.

He lay face up now, closed his eyes and tried not to dream at all.

Thursday, 16 July 1891, early afternoon

Sweating profusely, after another futile hour of searching for the gold bug, Dugas stepped over to the window to let air into Legrand's apartment. He slid the window open. As he reached for the shutters, he hesitated and peeked through the louvers. Four boys, sitting on the roof across the way, pointed at the window as Dugas cracked the louvers to look out.

Dugas slowly withdrew his hand and hurried out of the apartment. Racing around the corner, he made his way to St. Louis Street, locating the Creole townhouse directly behind Legrand's apartment house. He rushed up three flights of stairs to the hall dormer leading to the roof. Pausing to catch his breath, Dugas heard a door crack open behind him. Someone peeked out at him from one of the apartments.

He opened the lapel of his tan suit to show his badge. The door closed. The hall smelled of tomato gravy and garlic. Dugas pushed open the dormer's wide window and climbed out. He braced a foot on the gutter, reached around the pilaster and scaled the high pitched roof toward the boys sitting along the rooftop.

His foot slipped on the tiled roof and the boys saw him and scattered. Dugas got his footing and pressed on. One of the boys slipped and skidded toward Dugas who reached out and grabbed the boy's leg.

The boy froze.

Dugas pulled himself and the boy to the roof top and sat straddling the roof. Two of the boys jumped over the party wall dividing the building from the next townhouse. The fourth boy scampered the other way, around the brick chimney and over another party wall. In a moment all were gone, except the dark haired boy sitting next to Dugas.

The boy's dark brown eyes were the size of silver dollars, his little arms shook as he held on to the roof. The boy wore a red and white striped shirt and baggy gray shorts. He was barefoot and looked to be around eight years old.

"I'm a policeman," Dugas said, showing the boy his badge. "Policia. What's your name?"

Tears formed in the boys eyes.

Dugas tried smiling. "There's nothing to be afraid of. I just want to talk to you."

The boy started crying.

Dugas waited, feeling the sun hot on his head. A loud blast from a nearby ship caused him to look at the river. A steamboat passed a clipper ship along the big muddy water just beyond the levee, a couple hundred yards away.

When the crying diminished, Dugas pulled a handkerchief from his coat pocket and wiped the boy's face. Then he asked the boy his name.

"Salvatore," the boy said.

It took several minutes to discover the boy's full name was Salvatore Caprera, nine years old, who lived on Decatur Street. It took even longer to get the boy down to the dormer and into the hallway.

"Come along," he told the boy as he lead the lad down to the street.

Dugas led him up St. Louis to Chartres, holding on to the boy's collar. He pointed to the Third Precinct Police Station as they went past.

"You want to go there?"

Sal shook his head.

"Then come along."

Dugas led the boy to Toulouse Street, turning left, away from Legrand's apartment house to a small Creole sandwich shop called Lautrec's. He sat the boy at an inside table and positioned himself close to the door. He ordered croissants and coffee and cold milk for the boy. Salvatore was reluctant to eat even when Dugas prodded him, but once he tasted the freshly baked, warm croissants, he ate voraciously. Dugas ordered more coffee and a second milk.

When the boy finally seemed at ease, Dugas told him again he was not in trouble. He asked about the window the boys had been watching. He could see by the frightened look in the boy's eyes that this wouldn't be easy.

"What you saw is very important," he told the boy. "Very important." Dugas took out his note pad and pencil, placing them next to his coffee cup. Patiently, he questioned the boy and slowly, ever so slowly, the story came out.

Doctor Legrand, known to the boys only as the tall man, usually kept the window open when his visitors came. He turned on the electric light and lit candles. Most of the women stripped to the waist voluntarily, before he put the white cloth over their mouth and nose. Some of them took all of their clothes off. Legrand placed all of them on his bed and had his way with them. One woman would stand naked in the window brushing her hair after.

Yes, Sal remembered the dark haired girl last Monday, how Legrand opened the window and how she took all her clothes off, how Legrand cast a spell over her, then put the cloth over her mouth, how Legrand took off his clothes and climbed on her, how he got up later and hurriedly dressed, how he rushed out of the room and rushed back in later with a blue bottle in his hand. Fully clothed, Legrand climbed into bed with the woman. Later, he turned off the light and moved to the window and closed it.

Taking rapid notes, Dugas paused and asked, "What do you mean by putting a spell over them?"

"He swung a golden thing in front of them."

Looking at Sal's eyes, he carefully asked, "What did the man do with the golden thing after he had the women under his spell?"

"He hung it from the light."

The brass chandelier.

Thursday, 16 July 1891, late afternoon

It hung near the center of the brass chandelier between four glass bobbles, shimmering in the light from the bulbs around it. The size of a large pecan, the gold bug had six short legs and two jet-black spots on its back. The spots looked like eyes and the bug resembled a skull or death's head. It was no death's head, Dugas told himself, it was an Egyptian scarab, a golden beetle.

"Resurrection," Dugas told himself as he reached for it. In Ancient Egypt, the scarab stood for resurrection.

With trembling fingers, Dugas unwrapped the gold chain from the brass prong and climbed off the stack of books that Legrand had strategically placed beneath the chandelier. He examined the bug closely. Brushed to a brilliant gold, its weight told Dugas it was solid. The black spots were polished gemstones, onyx, just as Bridgette had described.

This piece of evidence was the final nail in Legrand's coffin. With this and testimony from Salvatore and the other boys, Dugas could expose Legrand, the charlatan, the fakir, the seducer of women, the murderer of Julie Maigret. The district attorney liked neat packages.

The more Dugas stared at the gold bug, the more beautiful it looked, the heavier it seemed to become. The longer he stared at it, the less sure he was that he even needed this. He had solved this case the moment he'd stepped into the room. Convicting Legrand would be the D.A.'s job. He wasn't judge and jury. Convicting Legrand would be easy for even the least experienced Assistant District Attorney, especially after the women from parish prison filed in to tell a good New Orleans jury how this charlatan took advantage of them. Terribly embarrassed at first, they were quite determined after Dugas spoke with them. It was an open and shut case.

Turning the gold bug over, letting it catch the light, rubbing his finger over it, Dugas felt its power. The cool metal warmed with his touch. Its brilliance shined so brightly he could barely look at it.

And suddenly, as if in a dream, she was there, standing in the doorway. Wearing a prim navy blue dress and matching hat, she stared at the gold bug in Dugas's hand. Slowly he extended his hand and let the bug dangle on its chain. Bridgette stepped in, closed the door and latched it. And even more slowly, she removed her hat, removed the pins from her hair and shook it out. Stepping closer, her gaze still riveted to the bug, she dropped her purse and began unbuttoning her dress.

Dugas's breathing grew deeper. Bridgette wore nothing beneath the dress. She stepped from it and moved to him, those blue eyes focused on the gold bug as if draw to it, like iron filings to a magnet. Her hands rose when she met Dugas and she pushed him slowly to the bed, her gaze still riveted on the gold bug. It occurred to the detective, as he fell into the sunlight to the bed, that he had opened the window when he had returned.

Dugas inhaled a deep whiff of her rose perfume. Bridgette reached for the golden chain, lifted it from his hand and draped it over his neck, letting the gold bug fall against his chest. Craning her neck forward, she kissed the bug, then his lips. Her eyes remained closed as she took long breaths between kisses. When they snapped open, Dugas saw a predatory look in them, more the look of a raptor than a woman. She reached for his belt buckle and quickly unfastened it.

She stood in front of him in her lovely nakedness and gasped, "The Gold Bug of Jean Lafitte. Put it over my neck." She leaned forward and Dugas sat up to drape the chain over her head. She straightened and the gold bug fell between the swell of her breasts. She climbed atop, shoving him back down and her eyes softened before she closed them for a long, deep, French kiss.

The passion was furious at first but slowed as they both wanted it to linger, to keep it from ending, to keep it going on and on until they could keep it going no longer and surrendered to it. Then they lay next to one another, both staring at the ceiling.

Rising finally, Bridgette pulled her hair back with one hand and kissed his lips softly. Standing on shaky legs, she crossed to her purse and pulled out a hair brush. She moved to the window and stood there brushing her long hair.

Dugas watched her as she brushed her hair, his breath slowly returning to normal. He suddenly remembered what Salvatore had said about one woman standing in the window brushing her hair.

Leaning to his left, he saw the side of Bridgette's pretty face. She was looking across to the roof where the boys had perched.

"Are they there?" he asked.

"Yes," she said in a deep, sexy voice. "Four of them watching me."

She took a couple steps back and did a slow pirouette for the boys. They she turned and faced them again. At that angle, they could see all of her. She remained there, brushing her hair. Dugas watched her. Although his eyelids felt heavy, he fought to keep them open, not wanting to miss a moment.

"You must keep the gold bug, monsieur." Bridgette looked over her shoulder at him. "You must keep it — for us."

Dugas's pulse rose and he felt his heart beating in his ears. Staring at those bright blue eyes, he knew, for the first time in his career, he would keep a piece of evidence. He would hide it behind the loose board in his bedroom wall, next to his bed.

"For us," she said. "You must keep it — for us."

Bridgette turned and walked slowly, languidly back to the bed.

"We must find another place to do this," she said, glancing around the room. "We can find one together, if you wish." Her voice was lower now, almost sad.

Dugas leaned up and kissed her again, felt her hand press against his chest and felt a tug on the gold chain.

Keep it for us, my darling.

Dugas pulled her to him and they made love again on the bed where her sister had died.

Friday, 17 July 1891, morning

Dugas woke to find he was alone. No Bridgette. No gold bug.

He went straight to St. Charles Avenue but the elderly woman would not see him. Alvin told him Madame Bridgette was gone and shut the door in Dugas's face. Dugas stepped away from the door, turned his face to the morning sun and closed his eyes, hoping the sun could ease the pain in his heart.

It was his partner, Patrick Shannon, who told Dugas the following day that Bridgette Madison had sailed to Paris. The big Irishman took Dugas aside in the Detective Office and in a low voice said, "She sailed on the *S.S. Lythotwytch.* Alone."

"How do you know this?"

Shannon shrugged. "I too am a detective, my friend. And I thought you'd want to know."

— As the days passed, and the long, lonely nights, Dugas felt the pain in his chest slowly diminish as he focused his energies on making certain the rogue Etienne Deschamps, better known as the magnetic murderer — Dr. Etienne Legrand, of Rue Toulouse — hanged by the neck until dead.

Guilty of Dust and Sin

Love bade me welcome;
yet my soul drew back,
Guilty of dust and sin.
    from *Love* by George Herbert (1583-1648)

An oblique shaft of sunlight, streaming through my office windows, illuminated the dust floating in the air and for a moment I was transported to that scene in *The Hunchback of Notre Dame* when beautiful Maureen O'Hara knelt in the cathedral with a beam of sunlight shining down on her from a high window, like a spotlight from God. In the black and white movie, the light was silver, here it's golden in the late morning.

Not that my office deserved any attention from God, unless it was a message to clean up the place. I had a broom, somewhere, probably in the closet next to the stove in the small kitchen area of my office.

Instead of digging it out, I kicked my feet up on my well-worn desk and opened the morning paper to read how General Eisenhower resigned his position as chief of staff of the army to become the Thirteenth President of Columbia University yesterday, June 6, 1948. June sixth, D-Day plus three years. Nice move, Ike.

Running footsteps drew my attention outside, where a boy's head rushed past my windows. Two seconds later, I heard the outer door bang open and a shadow move outside the smoky glass door of my office before the door flew open. He was about ten with wiry red hair and wore a striped tee-shirt, denims and black tennis shoes.

"Ain't you a detective?"

"Yeah." I moved the paper aside.

"You gotta come! There's a dead lady down the block."

He bounced in place as I crossed the office and pulled on my suit coat to cover my .38 Smith and Wesson in its leather holster on my right hip. I automatically looked at my Bulova, noting it was nine-fifteen.

"What's your name, son?"

"Alvin Rocke. What's yours?" He back-peddled out of the building.

"Lucien Caye."

"Well, hurry!" Alvin turned and ran up Barracks Street. I followed at a quick pace, but not running as I passed the stoops of the buildings abutting the sidewalk we call *banquettes* here in New Orleans because when it rained the streets of the lower French Quarter always flooded and the sidewalks became banks next to quick-flowing mini-canals.

Alvin stopped at the corner of Barracks and Burgundy, turned and looked back, waving me forward and pointing down Burgundy. When I reached the corner, Alvin was standing outside a wooden fence two houses from the intersection next to another boy, same age, this one with brown hair.

"We were tossing a football," Alvin said breathlessly, "and Joey threw it over the fence."

Joey shoved him. "I did not! You couldn't catch it. It bounced off your hands." Joey backed away from me as I stepped up. "Really, mister. Al can't catch worth a damn!"

The unpainted wooden fence was exactly my height, six feet. Alvin pointed to a cinder block. "I stood up on that and pulled myself up and that's when I saw her." He pressed his face against a crack in the fence and said, "She's still there."

I went up on the cinder block and looked over. She was still there all right, on her back, arms open wide, legs straight out. I pulled myself up and over the fence and dropped into a flower bed of azaleas. I took a long step to the concrete walkway next to the building and moved quickly to her.

Pressing two fingers against her carotid artery, I checked for a pulse even though she looked as dead as the GIs back on

Anzio beach, without the gore. Her face was dark, tongue
protruding from her mouth, eyes half opened in that dull look of
death. She was already cool.

"Alvin!"

"Yes, sir."

"Go to the grocery and tell Mr. Boudreaux to call the police
right away." Boudreaux's Grocery was at the next corner,
Burgundy and Esplanade Avenue.

"Ain't you a detective?"

"I'm a *private* detective. We need the police. Go get 'em."

"O.K." I heard Alvin tell Joey to stand guard and I almost
snickered.

"Is she dead?" It was Joey.

"Yeah. You wanna climb over and see?"

"No way!"

"Then stay there and flag down the cops when they get
here."

"O.K."

Still on my haunches, I studied the body. She looked to be
in her mid-thirties, a good five years older than me, with short,
strawberry blonde hair. A small shovel lay by her right hand, next
to three potted plants placed in the garden as if she was about to
plant them. Why would a woman work in her garden while
wearing a flashy red and yellow dress, stockings and red high
heels, her face made up as if she was about to go out on the town?

I took in a deep breath and smelled the flowers for the first
time, rich scents of azaleas and roses lining the wooden fence. I
examined her hands for defensive wounds. No wedding ring but
there was a gold ring with a nice ruby on the ring finger of her
right hand and bruises on the knuckles of her right hand, two red
fingernails broken off. She'd put up a fight all right. Leaning
closer to check the bruising around her throat, I saw a distinct
marking on her larynx, a half-moon crescent mark pressed deep
into her throat. She wasn't dragged through the garden. In fact,
she lay in an impression in the loose dirt as if she'd be held down,
strangled where she lay.

A car door slamming beyond the fence stood me up and that's when I spotted the crescent mark again, in the flower bed as if it just marched away from the body back toward the rear of the building.

Stepped back to the fence I came in the middle of the conversation between the man on the beat and excitable Alvin and Joey.

"Over here," I called out and waited for the beat cop to peer over the fence. It was Hutchings, mid-forties, balding with paunchy eyes.

"What you got Lucien?"

I stepped aside and said, "You'll need the detectives and the coroner."

"Jesus!" He blinked twice and stepped back to his car. I heard him calling for the dicks before returning to stand on the cinder block. I nodded to the building, which I could see was a double and asked if maybe he should knock.

"Good idea."

Hutchings was a good cop, not very imaginative, but we'd rode together before the war when I was so much younger, in a much younger world where violence was overseas, Europe and China. Hutchings was old enough to stay home while I joined the rangers and went to North Africa, Sicily and General Mark Clark's side show in Italy, until a damn German sniper took me down at Monte Cassino.

Alvin peeked over the fence and asked if I'd seen his football. I looked around and it was a good twenty yards beyond the body. I kept to the concrete walkway and picked it up, following the crescent marks that suddenly turned and moved up on the concrete, where I found one of the red fingernails. On my haunches again, I saw the muddy marks move away toward a back gate or maybe to the back doors of the building.

Looking back at the fence I saw Alvin's face peeking over and tossed him the ball, watching it bounce off his hands.

"What are you boys doing there?" I recognized the voice immediately and called out to Detective Walter Moncrief who looked a little like Basil Rathbone in his Sherlock Holmes persona, only Moncrief wore horn-rimmed glasses.

"Walter, they're the ones who found the body."

"Who's that?"

I told him and he asked what the hell I was doing there.

"Over here," Hutchings called out and Moncrief told me not to go anywhere as I heard him step away. I turned to the rear of the house and waited.

"Mr. Detective," Alvin called out.

"Yes?"

"Are we in trouble?"

"Not unless you killed this lady."

"No way!"

"Calm down, Alvin. And listen up. Did you or Joey see anyone on the street when y'all came around tossing your ball?"

"No, sir."

"You sure."

They both said they were as I spied Moncrief and Hutchings come around from the back of the building, a thick woman in heavy black dress behind them. The woman stopped, a white rag pressed against her mouth.

Moncrief wore one of his typical tweed suits, a pipe in his mouth, hair plastered down ala-Rathbone. You would take him for the cerebral detective, a regular Sherlock Holmes, until he spoke. He was soft-spoken all right, only his brain was too dull to be Sherlock or even a beat cop, much less a detective handling a homicide.

"Hello," he announced as he stepped up to the body (which reminded me of the old joke — How would you know Sherlock Holmes had stumbled onto to a triple murder? Answer — He goes, "Hallo. Hallo. Hallo.").

Moncrief took out his pipe and looked up at me. "What have we here?"

"Dead woman," I deadpanned.

He was a good two inches shorter than me and weighed a good fifty pounds less, which made him a scarecrow of a man because I was lean enough.

"So what have you to do with all this?"

So I told him, even pointing out the crescent marks. He nodded and asked me to step outside with the boys and wait while he examined the crime scene. I shrugged and went toward the back of the building.

"Don't forget this fingernail." I stopped and pointed down to the nail.

"What fingernail?"

The woman still had a rag in her mouth, her face streaming tears. I took her elbow and led her back to the open door at the rear of the building. The other door, I noted was closed. I sat the woman at her kitchen table and took her hand. She came around a minute later, wiping the tears with the rag.

"Is she?"

"Yes, ma'am. Who is she?"

The woman stood and straightened her dress and asked if I'd like some coffee. I put her over forty with mousy brown hair showing streaks of gray.

"Coffee would be nice."

The kitchen smelled of pine sol and baked bread. As she filled two cups of coffee she told me her name was Alice Walker and the deceased was renting the other side of her double. "Her name is Phyllis Bantry. She's lived here ten years."

"She married?"

"No." Alice put a cup and saucer in front of me and we both sat.

The coffee was weak, glad I decided to drink it black, but Phyllis's story was interesting enough to make up for it. A war widow, husband killed at Iwo Jima, Phyllis reverted back to her maiden name since she didn't have children. Her husband's name was Isoslavitch and Phyllis would often joke, through tears, how she always had a hard time spelling it.

Phyllis was a vivacious woman at thirty-five, always dressed up, often working in her garden in high heels, stockings and evening dress. She always wore make-up.

"She have a boyfriend?"

"A number of them." Alice looked away. "Most recently one. Thomas Knowlton, lives on Esplanade up by City Park. He's a vet too. Has to walk with a cane."

"Was he around this morning?"

Alice shrugged, tears welling up just as Moncrief poked his head in and asked to use the phone. Spotting me, he said, "What are you doing in here?" As if I had my hand up Alice's dress or something.

Moncrief ordered me to go out and make sure those boys hadn't disappeared. When I worked the Third Precinct here in the Quarter and Moncrief worked the uptown at the Seventh District on Magazine Street, I heard he was often too bossy for his britches. Glad to see he hadn't changed.

Alvin and Joey were tossing the football with two negro kids, another Joey and an Eddie, all out in the middle of narrow Burgundy Street. Alvin ran to me immediately, proudly telling the new kids who I was. I sat on the front stoop and told them about the crime scene until they grew bored and asked if I'd mind playing quarterback.

"None of us got an arm."

I took off my suit coat and tossed a few. We had to move out of the way of the coroner's wagon. Just as I hit Eddie with a down-and-out next to the fire hydrant, Moncrief came out and yelled, "Caye! What the hell're you doing now?"

"A down-and-out."

He scowled at the kids, then told me he needed a formal statement from me.

"Sure. What about the kids who found the body?"

"Yeah. Which ones are they?"

As I said, dull brain and not very observant.

#

By the time I returned to my office from downtown, Thomas Knowlton was a wanted man. I watched Moncrief build his case against Knowlton, first at the corner's office and then as I sat in the uncomfortable wooden chair next to his desk in the Detective Bureau.

The autopsy of Phyllis Bantry, white female, thirty-five, 5'1" tall, weighing one hundred pounds, was quick and to the point. She'd been killed that morning between six and eight a.m. The cause of death was strangulation, which included a collapsed larynx. The manner of death — homicide. I wasn't sure why Moncrief had me tag along, except to show me how the big boys did it. Thomas Knowlton couldn't be found by the patrol officers sent to locate him at his Esplanade Avenue apartment, three blocks from City Park.

Puffing his pipe as he sat behind his desk, filling the office with the thick scent of tobacco laced with some sort of spice, Moncrief determined the crescent marks had come from the bottom of Knowlton's cane. Deductive reasoning, claimed Moncrief.

"We'll find him and we'll find his walking stick and it will have a cap on the bottom with a half-moon imprint."

This guy should be a writer, I thought. There were plenty science-fiction magazines out there.

"What if you find his cane and there's no half-moon cap?"

"Then he has another cane that he's hidden."

Why hadn't I thought of that? I nodded, as if impressed and Moncrief smiled for the first time today. Then he sent me home in a prowl car as he led the way to Knowlton's with a search warrant.

Returning to my office, I found a woman sitting on the hall sofa, hands folded in her lap, large green eyes staring at me as I walked in. She stood as I moved to my office door and said, "Hello Lucien. Do you remember me?"

She wore a high-collared black dress, long and full, and black heels. She had sultry good looks, probably in her late-thirties, five-eight, maybe one-forty, her light brown hair pinned on the sides with silver barrettes. Her mouth was a little too large, full lips with a hint of brick red lipstick. It was when she smiled, that familiar sad smile, I recognized her.

"Miss Arcola?" I felt my face light up as I realized this was my eighth grade teacher from Holy Rosary. It came back to me in snap shots, flashes of her coming into the classroom for the first time, a pretty young woman with bright eyes.

"Call me Marie," she said holding a trembling hand for me to shake.

"Are you O.K.?"

"I need your help." Her lower lip quivered.

I led her in and crossed the office to my desk, her heels echoing behind me on the hard wood. Marie Arcola was my first crush, my first bout of unrequited love watching her talk and move around the classroom, realizing there was a female body beneath her clothes, something I'd never thought about the nuns. They were too mean to be female. Oh, how I remembered those painful, heart-palpitating days.

Marie sat in one of the chairs in front of my desk, crossing her legs and I noticed her heels weren't high heels, but sensible low heels and also noticed her dress was old-fashioned, pre-war.

"Can I get you some coffee?"

"*May* I?" She corrected me, that sad smile again. "No, thank you."

I went and sat behind my desk, took out a pad and pen and looked back at her. "What can I do for you?"

"I have a friend in trouble." Her voice shook. "With the police." She took a handkerchief from her small purse and dabbed her eyes. I waited.

"His name is Thomas Knowlton and he's a veteran like you."

I kept my voice low and soft so it wouldn't sound like an interrogation. "How do you know him?"

"He's been a … beau … for a while." She looked at the window. "We weren't serious." She took in a deep breath. "What

he wanted I wasn't ready to give until ... marriage. You know
what I mean, Lucien." That last sentence was in her teacher voice.
"So he found another for that, but we still saw one another ..."
Her green eyes glistened as she looked at me, blinked and sent
tears streaming. She pressed the handkerchief against her eyes.

I waited until she recovered to say, "Phyllis Bantry, right?"

Her eyes became wide and she sat back in the chair. "Do
you know her?"

I shook my head and told her about finding the body. Her
shoulders sank and it took her a minute to compose herself.

"Phyllis moved two doors from me a couple years ago and
was so friendly to everyone in the neighborhood. I didn't realize
how friendly to Thomas until about six months ago." She wiped
her eyes again.

"The police came asking about Thomas and told me what
happened to that Bantry woman." She sat up straighter. "I want
you to find Thomas before the police do because they may hurt
him and I know he didn't do what they say."

"How do you know that?"

"I know Thomas."

"I mean, was he with you this morning?"

She shook her head. "I go to mass every morning. Our
Lady of Guadaloupe. Six o'clock mass. Thomas never rises that
early."

"Do you have any idea where he could be?"

For the next fifteen minutes, I took notes. Thomas
Knowlton lived in a small apartment house on Esplanade, corner of
Leda and drove a 1941 Ford coupe. They'd met at the public
library. I watched her as she spoke, the bright sunlight on her face
when the sun peeked out from behind a cloud. There were age
lines beginning around her mouth and eyes but she was still a
pretty woman, dressed a little old fashioned but still, she was my
first crush.

"Why does he use a cane?" I asked.

She told me he was wounded badly in the war and lived on his veterans disability. "He almost lost his left leg and was so shell shocked, they sent him home."

"Where was this?"

"Anzio."

I felt the hairs standing on the back of my neck.

"His cane," I said, "ever notice a cap onthe bottom of the cane?"

She gave me a puzzled look.

I cleared my throat and asked her to tell me about her neighbors. "You said Phyllis was friendly with your neighbors, right?" If I was going to do this, I was going to do it right. Talk to everyone. Maybe someone saw something.

When I was out of questions, we both stood and I walked her to the door. She turned, close enough for me to catch a whiff of her light perfume and said, "I read what the paper said about you at Monte Cassino, receiving the silver star and being wounded."

So that's how she knew I was a vet.

She put a friendly hand on my chest, gave me another of those sad smiles and left. I watched her walk past the windows back up toward Burgundy Street to her house around the corner.

I've said it before. New Orleans was nothing more than a big small town.

#

Don't know why I bothered canvassing when they kept coming to me.

After talking to everyone in the neighborhood, I returned to find a middle-aged man sitting on the foyer's sofa. He needed his cane to stand up.

"You Lucien Caye?"

I nodded. "You must be Thomas Knowlton."

"Yep." He was six feet tall, like me, around two-hundred pounds, with short brown hair, a thin moustache on a pale face and wide-spaced eyes that were probably hazel. Dapper in a three-piece seersucker blue suit, dark blue tie with a white dress shirt and two-toned black and white loafers.

We shook hands firmly and I invited him into my office. When he sat and leaned his cane against my desk, I scooped it up and looked at the hard-rubber cap and there was no half-moon symbol on the bottom.

"You have another one of these?"

"No. It's army issue."

It looked it, plain wood with a plain rubber cap. I put it down and went around and sat behind my desk. He didn't look worried, even when I said, "You have a problem, Mr. Knowlton."

"Since the war, that's all I've had."

"You need a good lawyer and you have to turn yourself in."

He looked around my office and stopped at the windows and we both watched the afternoon sunlight streaming in, again illuminating dust in the air, but it had no heavenly glow this time. It was more like the light of accusation falling on his pasty face.

"I didn't kill Phyllis," he said with a catch in his voice, turning to me with eyes narrowed.

"How'd you hear about it?"

He looked at the windows again. "Huh?"

"It wasn't in the afternoon newspaper." I'd checked it out when I stopped for a soft drink at Boudreaux's Grocery during my canvass. "So how'd you hear about Phyllis?"

He blinked at me. "Marie told me. That's when she said I should come to see you."

He kept blinking and looking around. It didn't take a genius to see he was having trouble focusing.

"I've been asking around and so far no one saw anyone near Phyllis's, not even you, which is good," I told him. "The police find a witness who can put you near the scene this morning, you're as good as electrified." That was the politest way I could describe what cop call the 'hot squat' in Louisiana's infamous electric chair.

He nodded slowly.

"So, where were you this morning between six and eight?"

"Home. Sleeping."

"Anybody see you there, call you on the phone, see you leave?"

He shook his head.

"So, is there anything you can tell me about Phyllis? Any enemies? Anyone who would kill her?"

"No."

And it went like that for the next half hour. Me asking questions, him giving me one word responses until I asked about Anzio. He leaned back and told me it was hell on earth. "I was supposed to be behind the line. Signal Corps. I was a radioman. But the Krauts brought up those big guns ..."

My turn to nod. "I know. I was there."

"Really?"

"Ranger battalion. Trapped under those big guns for God knows how long." Sometimes, when it rained like the devil here in New Orleans, when the lightning danced and thunderclaps shook the old buildings here in the Quarter, I'd brake into a cold sweat. It was like Field Marshal Kesselring bringing up his siege cannon again to rain hellfire on us.

"Almost lost my leg," Knowlton said in a wavering voice. "They let me out on a section eight. Shell shock. At least I get disability pay."

I didn't want to grill him but I had to ask about his relationship with Phyllis Bantry. He told me, man to man, it was sexual. She was a 'wildcat', but he didn't say it bragging or anything like that. When I asked about Marie Arcola, he looked at the windows again.

"She's saving herself for that knight in shining armor." His voice caught. "Sure ain't me."

I asked if he knew a lawyer and he didn't so I suggested one.

#

Like I said, they kept coming back. When I returned from watching Thomas Knowlton turn himself in, Marie Arcola was waiting, standing in the foyer, this time in a dark blue dress, dark blue barrettes in her hair, same shoes.

"Have you seen Thomas?"

"Yes," I told her as I unlocked my office door and held it open for her. I waited until we were both seated to tell her Knowlton had just turned himself in.

"But what's going to happen to him?"

I told her about the lawyer, a former-cop, who was a pretty good defense attorney and his advice to Knowlton, which was pretty basic. Don't talk to the cops.

She was worried he'd be hurt in jail.

"It's jail, not a torture chamber," I assured her, knowing better. Parish Prison was pretty rough but the jailers would know he was a disabled veteran and that should count for something.

"I'm going to work on the case for Thomas," I said. "Starting with his neighbors. See if anyone saw him leave home after eight a.m. When did you talk to him today?"

She seemed surprised.

"Did you tell him about Phyllis?"

"Oh, yes. He called me around noon. You were outside talking to the neighbors and I told him."

"How did he react?"

"He couldn't believe it. He started crying."

The late afternoon sunlight on her face made her look twenty again and I felt my heart beating faster as we talked. We went back for a little while, back to the bricks of Holy Rosary School to her first year teaching, my last year in grammar school, and for a moment I was sitting behind a school desk, daydreaming of those green eyes, those full lips, that slim body.

She thanked me as she stood and told me I didn't need to walk her out. As she moved away a beam of sunlight streamed through the windows, another spotlight effect and I watched the dust rise from where she walked. Jesus, it was so thick Marie's shoes left impressions.

I followed her and when she stopped with the door open and turned back I stepped up. She stared up into my eyes and I moved closer and didn't stop my face from closing in on her, my mouth inching to those pouty lips.

She pressed a finger against my lips, stopping me, gave me that sad smile and left me with my heart thundering. I closed the door and turned back to my empty office with its dust particles floating and went to the closet for the broom. It was the sunlight again, that caused me to stop and bend over and look at the impressions left by Marie's shoes. I sat heavily on my dirty floor and stared at the neat, crescent impressions, little half-moon dust marks on the hardwood floor.

I remembered Thomas Knowlton's shoes as the jailers removed them. Well worn soles with no cap on the heel, nothing that would leave a crescent impression. Leaning back on my hands I stared out my office windows as the sun sank in the western sky, casting long shadows over Cabrini Playground across Barracks Street.

So what now?

Telling a detective he arrested the wrong man never set well, probably worse for someone who thought he was Sherlock Holmes. There was only one thing I could do. I left the broom on the floor and locked up my office, climbing upstairs to my apartment to lay on my sofa to figure out how I was going to get her to confess.

It wasn't a dream actually, but later, as I lay there, I saw it played out in scenes. Marie holding hands with Thomas Knowlton, Marie pulling away when he moved toward her, Thomas meeting a vivacious Phyllis, kissing her, following her into her bedroom. Then I saw the rage inside Marie Arcola and saw her standing over Phyllis Bantry and grinding the heel of her shoe into the small woman's throat.

#

Our Lady of Guadaloupe, the oldest church in New
Orleans, was once a mortuary chapel where victims of the great
yellow fever epidemic of 1826 were passed on their way to the
cemeteries. Built of bricks and Louisiana cypress covered by gray
masonry, it was a typical colonial chapel, a long rectangle with tall
archways and a bell tower with a cross atop. I parked my pre-war
1940 DeSoto coach on Rampart Street, right in front of the church
at 6:15 a.m. and went in just as the priest finished his sermon and
was stepping back to the alter.

It took a minute to spot Marie Arcola kneeling in the third
pew, a white embroidered cover atop her head. There were only a
handful in the church, all women, none paying attention to the slim
man standing at the back of church. And as I waited for mass to
end, the strong scent of burning candles and incense took me back
to a case last year, a case that had me in that same church.

It was a wandering father case that brought a little boy to
my office, asking me to find his dad who has crawled into a beer
bottle. Plenty of beer bottles. Stepping to my right, I looked into
an alcove, at a stature of a medieval fellow, maybe twenty years
old with wavy brown hair. He was in a serf costume, baggy green
shirt, brown leather vest, brown pants, brown high top sandals and
a plum colored cape. He held a cross in his right hand. Beneath
the statue was a small plaque that read, 'St. Expedite. Pray for us'.

Only in New Orleans would people pray to a non-existent
saint. When that particular statue arrived from Europe, God knows
when, with other statues properly marked St. Jude and St. Joseph,
the only marking on the crate carrying this statue was the word
'expedite' and so the workers unpacking the crate wrote St.
Expedite on the order form for the plaque and another New
Orleans legend was born. By the time the archbishop of New
Orleans discovered the mistake, too many New Orleanians had
said too many prayers to St. Expedite to remove the plaque. And
they still prayed to a saint that never was.

Eventually the mass ended and I watched the women leave,
all except Marie Arcola who still knelt in the third pew with her
head bowed. There was sunlight streaming in through the high

widows above, but this was no movie scene. The place was too
clean for dust in the air and Marie was no innocent-eyed Maureen
O'Hara praying for the poor.

She didn't even hear me walk up the aisle and slide into the
pew next to her. Hunched over in prayer, chin pressed against
clasped hands which held a white rosary, eyes closed tight, she
remained motionless until I said, "You haven't gone to confession
yet, have you?"

She jumped to her left, hands on the pew in front of her to
keep from tumbling over. She looked around quickly.

"We're alone. 'Cept for Him, of course." I nodded to the
big crucifix behind the alter.

Her right hand went to her throat as she stared at me with
saucered eyes.

"You were the only one who didn't go to communion."
Besides me, of course.

She tried to recover, giving me Bambi eyes, giving me that
'what, little ole' me?' look, but it didn't work.

"I know why you haven't gone to confession yet."

Slowly, she sat back on the pew, away from me, staring
with green frightened eyes.

"Too hard to put into words? What will the Father think?"

She finally took in a deep breath, arms folded now across
her chest as she lean further away from me.

"If you don't confess, there's no absolution. No
communion. But you know that. Just like I know you killed
Phyllis."

She gasped, hand covering her mouth, rosary dangling like
spittle from a corpse.

"Wasn't easy was it, standing over her and watching her
face turn red then purple?"

I could see the recognition in her eyes.

"You're a good six, seven inches taller than Phyllis, out-
weighed her by a good forty pounds." She recoiled as if I'd
slapped her. A southern gentleman never mentioned a woman's
weight, then again I'm a detective, not a gentleman.

She sank back in the pew, looked at Jesus up on the cross and made the sign of the cross. She closed her eyes and her lips moved in a silent prayer. It was short, maybe an "Our Father" before she looked at me again.

"I'm going to the police," I told her. "I think you should come along."

I held my hand out and she took it. I waited for her to genuflect then walked with her out to my DeSoto. I could hear the metal clip of her heels on the tile floor. Opening the passenger door for her, I let her in, then reached down and took off her right shoe, turned it over and spied the silver cap on the heel, a crescent shape, a half moon that made such neat impressions.

She gave me a fearful, puzzled look when I handed the shoe back.

Climbing behind the wheel, I looked at her again. She was staring out the windshield.

"How did you find out?" she asked.

"It's what I do," I turned on the ignition. "I'm a detective."

The Desire Streetcar

There still is a streetcar named Desire, but it doesn't run anymore. It just sits at the end of the old French Market, next to the dilapidated U.S. Mint, across the street from the rat infested wharves along the Mississippi River. It rests at the edge of what is now a flea mart. Vendors at the flea mart use the streetcar to lean their wares against.

No one rides the Desire Streetcar anymore. In fact, no one can even get inside, because it's boarded up. People can look at it, take an occasional picture of it as they visit the run-down antique shops and dusty bookstores nearby.

Now that's hardly a fitting end to a legendary streetcar, yet someone thought it should be there, with all the other junk, just as someone else thought the streetcar was a fitting place to deposit the mutilated body of a prostitute one night. That someone propped the prostitute's nude, mangled body in one of the seats, then carefully boarded the streetcar back up again before leaving.

As usual, there were no witnesses. No one saw it happen nor heard anyone breaking in or boarding up the streetcar after. No one even noticed what was inside, until two nights later when an old black couple noticed an inordinate number of rats running around the streetcar. The old man wiped the grime away from one of the windows and peeked in. He caught sight of what was attracting the rats, fell away from the window and puked.

On that hot, muggy, spring New Orleans night, with the humidity so thick you could feel it pressing against your face like a hot rag, I was awakened from my air-conditioned sleep by a phone call. It was my partner, Stan. He told me to meet him down by the Desire Streetcar because we had to identify the body of a girl we knew.

"What?"

"Just fuckin' meet me," he said in a distant, low voice and hung up.

Stan was waiting for me, pacing in front of the streetcar. He looked a mess. Unshaven, his usually meticulously groomed blond hair was matted and wet from sweat. The muscle-shirt and jeans he wore looked as if he'd pulled them from a dirty clothes hamper. I knew I didn't look much better in my jogging shorts and PANO tee-shirt.

Stan looked away from my eyes when I stepped up, scratched the pavement with his tennis shoe and said, "I knew it. I just fuckin' knew it."

There were homicide men in the streetcar, along with crime lab technicians. Two more homicide men were interviewing an old black couple a few feet away. I sucked in a deep breath and almost gagged at the stench in the air. I recognized the pungent, sharp smell. Blood, I was smelling rotten blood.

Inching toward the front of the streetcar, I watched flashlights from the homicide men bathe a body propped up in one of the seats. Her face was gone, her neck and shoulders were swollen black and gray, yet I knew who it was by the strands of long blond hair still clinging from bloody clumps atop her head. I moved away and sat on the curb. Resting my elbows on my knees, I craned my head forward and closed my eyes.

When she'd disappeared three days earlier, Stan instinctively knew. He said we'd find her in pieces. Fuck if he wasn't right. I heard him tell the same thing to the Homicide dicks that night. Mumbled responses from the detectives echoed from the streetcar. The words . . . 'whore . . . snitch . . . rats', along with a host of 'mother-fucks' and one loud 'fuck-this-shit'.

I had trouble breathing the super-heated air. A gust of wind, straight from the streetcar, passed over me, causing me to retch and place my head between my knees for a moment. Standing, I felt my stomach bottom out as I watched two coroner's assistants carry out the black body bag. They were followed by several large rats. One of the detectives drop kicked a rat, careening it off the side of the streetcar.

One of the dicks, who'd been talking to Stan, patted my partner on the shoulder and said, "Don't let it get to you. We see shit like this every fuckin' day."

He didn't say she was just a whore, but that's what he meant.

Yes, there still is a streetcar named Desire, but it no longer runs down Desire Street, no longer runs through the Faubourg Marigny past Frenchmen Street and Marais, St. Roch and St. Claude, Music and Esplanade, Burgundy and Dauphine Streets, Piety and, of course, Elysian Fields. It just sits now.

#

She was perched on a bar stool in the Rumboogie Bar, block of St. Claude Avenue, a block from Elysian Fields. I spotted her long, straight blond hair through the open door of the bar. She wore tight white jeans and a yellow tee-shirt with the words 'NICE GIRL' in glitter across her chest. Nursing a beer, she looked bored on a Tuesday night that was well on its way into Wednesday morning — four a.m.

Stepping in, I realized she and I were the only two white people in the place. A fat black man was shooting pool at the lone table. A even fatter black whore was leaning on the bar, talking to a bartender with a flat top and a hideous scar on the right side of his face. I could see him gleek me over the top of his sunglasses as I walked in and sat two stools away from the blond girl.

Sporting a three-day-old beard, I wore an old fatigue shirt and some well worn jeans that covered the ankle holster on my left ankle, where I kept my new .357 magnum Smith and Wesson Model 66 revolver. I had a .22 magnum Derringer in my waistband for quick retrieval, and a four inch razor-sharp dagger in a sheath that I wore on my hip, under my fatigue shirt. I ordered a beer and waited.

A minute later, she said, "What does the red one mean on your patch?" She had a real country-ass Mississippi accent.

I didn't look at her as I answered, "First Infantry Division."

"You're a Marine?"

"Hardly. I was a dogface."

"A what?"

"I was Regular Army."

She leaned an elbow on the bar and said, "Why you call yourself dogface? You got a cute moustache."

"You ever see an infantryman in combat? Looks just like a dog lost in the rain."

She moved to the stool next to mine. She didn't look half bad in the dark, a little skinny and used, but I'd seen worse. "What combat were you ever in?"

"Vietnam."

"You too young to been in Vietnam."

"I got in the ass-end of the war." Hell, the last Marines just left that goddamn country three years ago. Guess she didn't watch the evening news much.

"What's your name, soldier?" she asked as she put a hand on my shoulder.

"Dino. What's yours?"

"Xanthe." She blinked her light green eyes at me.

I had to force back a smile. "Where'd you pick up that name, Bourbon Street?"

"Ma momma give me that name."

"Sure. That's a common name in Mississippi, isn't it?"

She smiled. "All right. So I made it up. I like the way it sounds."

I bought her a draft, and she told me her real name was Thelma Wortling until she arrived in picturesque New Orleans from the backwoods of Mississippi and decided she needed a name as sexy as her new home town. She told me she was nineteen. She looked older. She said she used to live on a hog farm ten miles outside Jackson. Now, she lived in a one room apartment above a born again Christian book store on St. Claude Avenue.

"Turning tricks on top a religious book store turns me on," she said three beers later, as I followed her into her apartment. She plopped down on a mattress that lay in the middle of the room and started unfastening her jeans.

"Don't do that," I said as I looked around the room at the small refrigerator that appeared older than I was, at the tiny dining room table, yellowed with age, and its matching chair, equally yellow and worn. There was a lamp on the floor next to the mattress and a closet with no doors, where she hung her wardrobe, such as it was. There was no window.

"Well then what you got in mind, soldier?"

"I want to talk."

"You wanna talk 'fuck talk'?"

"No, I wanna talk you into helping me," I said as I stood uneasily at the edge of her mattress. I reached into my pocket, pulled out a twenty and dropped it in her lap. She gave me a strange look as she tucked it in her pocket.

"You gonna tell me what this is about?" she asked.

"You hungry?"

"Sure," she said, zipping up her jeans. She got up quickly. "After I go to the little girl's room." She stepped over to the small bathroom and closed the door. I took a deep breath and waited, still trying to figure out how to ask her, how to get her to help me.

I opened the apartment door and let in some fresh air. When she came bouncing out of the bathroom, I said, "There's an all night place down on Rampart that serves good Italian."

"You mean Aunt Gennie's?"

She knew the place. She seemed nervous, but wasn't about to turn down a good meal. I was hungry myself, from not eating right lately, and felt better when we slipped into our chairs in the small restaurant.

Aunt Gennie's, even after five in the morning, smelled delicious. It smelled of red gravy and garlic bread. The waiter, a tall gay with a green streak in his crew cut hair, was perky and friendly. Probably just came on duty.

Xanthe asked me to order for her, so I ordered. After our bread arrived, I broke off a piece and got to the subject. "Do you have any brothers?"

"Yeah. One." Xanthe spread a thick swatch of butter on her Italian bread. "Real bastard. Fucked me when I was twelve. Then let his friends fuck me for five dollars apiece." She smiled as she said it, rolling her eyes. "Actually, I *liked* his friends." She took a bite of bread and shrugged her shoulders.

"What's this?" she asked when our dinners arrived.

"Tortellini. It's like ravioli."

"Only kinda Italian food I eat is spaghetti. Even here." She shoved in a mouthful and made a yummy sound.

I dug into my own tortellini. It was very good.

"You Italian?" she asked.

"Sicilian."

"Oh, the mean kind."

"You can say that."

She downed a gulp of vino before asking, "You got any brothers?"

This girl wasn't stupid.

"I had a brother."

"What happened to him?"

"He was murdered."

She paused a moment, her fork in mid-air. "Really?"

"He was shot to death. By a burglar. He was a policeman."

"Wow," her green eyes widened. "There was a cop killed right next to where I live a couple months ago."

My eyes must have given me away as I stared at her. I watched as she slowly realized. "Oh," she said, leaning back in her chair. I could see her mind clicking behind her eyes. She had soft eyes, or maybe it was the lighting in the restaurant, softer than I'd expected of a Fifth District whore.

I went back to my supper and watched her. She ate a lot, jumped at dessert when offered. Then again, she was so thin. I had a cappuccino while she finished off a healthy slice of lemon meringue pie. After, I took her for a ride up Rampart to Canal Street, then up to City Park Avenue where I parked my Volkswagen.

"I wanna show you a secret I learned when I was a kid," I told her as I climbed out. I stepped over to a narrow opening between the fence and the wall of St. Patrick's Cemetery. "My brother showed me this," I said as I slipped into the cemetery.

She was still in the car, watching me. I put my hands up on the fence and told her to come. She hesitated. I turned and walked into the cemetery. It took a minute, but she finally followed, stumbling on the uneven brick walkway and stammering, "Don't leave me like that."

"We used to play hide and seek here when I was a kid."

"You kiddin'?" She put a hand on my shoulder. "This gives me the creeps."

"It safe at night, except for the ghosts."

"Don't say that." Her hand squeezed the top of my shoulder.

I led the way to a marble tombstone with a New Orleans star-and-crescent badge on it. The tombstone read:

Joseph Anthony LaStanza
IN THE LINE OF DUTY

I must have talked an hour. It told her about the sock hops, about sitting in the bleachers while my big brother, in his leather jacket, danced with the teen-aged girls who looked like movie stars to me. I told her about magical nights watching Morgus The Magnificent on television, back when werewolves prowled City Park and vampires crept from the Canal Cemeteries. I even told her how King Kong lived along the batture, behind the Audubon Park levee. I took her to the edge of the cemetery and showed her another cemetery called Odd Fellow's Rest.

"My brother told me dwarfs and cripples were buried in there."

Xanthe was a good listener.

"Actually," I said, taking her hand and leading her back through St. Patrick's, "Odd Fellow's is a seafarer's society."

When we slipped back out, she took my hand again and gave me a peck on the cheek. "I thought you had something kinky in mind," she said, nodding back to the cemetery. Whatever perfume she was wearing was nice. It wasn't strong, but nice up close.

On the way back, I propositioned her. I told her I needed her help. When I showed her my badge and ID, she said she knew I was a cop the minute I walked into the Rumboogie Bar.

"But you can't be Vice. There's all old, fat bastards."

It was daylight by the time I dropped her off around the corner from the born-again Christian book store. She leaned in the passenger window and said, "You sure you don't wanna come up for a minute?"

"No," I said. "Let's keep this all business."

"It's always business with me," she said with a big smile. She ran her tongue over her lips.

"You sure about Thursday morning?" I asked again, reminding her of our next date.

"Yeah. I take a cab to the Mardi Gras fountain, wherever the hell that is. Meet you at six a.m." She shifted her weight from one leg to the other and ran her hand through her long hair. "You just let me work at it. If the word's out here on the street . . . Xanthe the blond will find out." She walked away slowly and seductively around the corner.

#

"Never fuck an informant," was the first thing Jack Blanc told me when I told him about Xanthe. "If you fuck 'em, they got something on you. They got a piece of you. And I don't mean a little dick, either."

Sergeant Jack Blanc was a legend on the department and an outcast. He became a legend years earlier when he single-handedly tracked down and killed the man who'd killed his partner. Then Jack went to the killer's funeral and pumped a few extra rounds into the killer's body as it lay in the coffin, much to the horror of the killer's family. Jack Blanc was known, from then on, as the man who got his man — twice.

Jack was fired over that little incident, not because he shot a cadaver, but because he made the mistake of shooting through the American flag draped over the killer's casket. Jack took the department to court and won a landmark decision that forced the department to treat officers for stress. Stress caused Jack to shoot the American flag, nothing more.

Jack was reinstated and immediately became an outcast to anyone above the rank of patrolman. How he got promoted to sergeant, no one knows. How he managed to get banished to the Bloody Sixth District was easy to understand. Jack Blanc was the only man in the history of the New Orleans Police Department to have been assigned to *every* district, every division, every unit on the department — except Internal Affairs, which goes without saying. They saved the Sixth District for last.

Jack was a city slick Coon-Ass, a relocated Louisiana bayou Frenchman come to the big city. He had a large black moustache that matched his mat of curly black hair, and a dark, olive face marked by that craggy Cajun complexion of south Louisiana. He looked like a young Caesar Romero, only larger in the chest and arms.

"So," Jack said, readjusting the ever-present cigar in his mouth, "what the fuck is Homicide doing about your brother's murder anyway?"

"You got me," I answered, leaning against the fender of my marked unit as we stood outside the old Cotton Exchange Building on Jackson Avenue.

"So, now you figure you'd work on the case on your own."

"Stan's gonna help." I nodded to my partner, who was just climbing out of our marked unit and stretching.

"It's a fuckin' shame," Jack said. "An unsolved murder of a New Orleans policeman." He growled as he exhaled a large cloud of smoke. "Who the fuck ever *heard* of such a thing?"

"Yeah," I said, half under my breath.

"OK," Jack said, "so, we solve it."

"Fuckin' Ay," Stan yelled, nodding fiercely. After a few seconds, he stopped nodding and asked Jack, "OK, how do we do it?"

Jack looked around and sniffed the air like a coon-dog. "It's out there," he said. "The solution's out there. All we gotta do is find it."

Stan slapped me on the back and said, "See. Told you he used to work Homicide." He looked back at Jack and said, "OK, so how do we do it?"

Jack took a long puff on his cigar, which gave me time to inject, "I got a whore working on it already."

That's when I told them what I meant about informants earlier, when I asked Jack about fucking an informant. I told them about Xanthe and how she was already pumping the locals for information, literally. When I finished, Jack added a postscript to the evening's conspiracy. He said we were gonna kill my brother's killer. "Then maybe we'll shoot up a coffin, OK?"

"Fuckin' Ay," Stan said.

#

The Mardi Gras Fountain was isolated between the levee and Lake Pontchartrain. You could only get to it by way of Lakeshore Drive. I parked my VW and waited atop the levee behind the fountain. I passed the time watching the purple, gold and green lighted water bubbling in the fountain. At ten minutes after six, a cab pulled up. Xanthe got out and started toward me. Atop the levee, I had a clear view of the entire area.

"When do I get to see you in your cute little uniform?" she asked as she sat in front of me in the early morning light. She wore a tight red dress that was split up the front all the way to the bottom of her white panties. She hiked her skirt as she sat crossed legged, facing me, making sure I had a clear view of her crotch. "Figured you'd enjoy this view better than the lake," she said. Xanthe did have sleek legs and nice full hips and knew how to show off both.

I could see she was excited. I thought she was probably on something until she said, "Word on the street is that it was two dudes that killed your brother. A nigger from the Desire Projects, and a spick. The spick's been bragging about it."

I felt my breath slip away.

"The detectives have been all over the place," she added, "but they don't know shit. I got a date with a dude in a couple days who knows the spick. I'm gonna pump him for all he'll give me." She smiled and batted those green eyes at me. She looked different, all dolled up that way, with strands of her hair moving in the lake breeze, with her face made up and dark red lipstick. She wasn't a bad looking girl, on the nasty side of things.

She leaned back on her hands and told me just how she planned to get the information. "I'll use my lips. All four of them." She reached her left hand down to the front of her panties and toyed with their silky edge. "Damn hair's always sticking out the sides," she said in a mock complaint. I could see her green eyes watching me as she moved her panties around, revealing the dark pubic hair beneath. She left some of the hair sticking out the sides of her panties when she finished. I looked back at her face as she twisted her neck and tossed her long hair to one side. She was grinning at me like that *Alice In Wonderland* cat.

I passed her the envelope with the money I'd taken from my credit union account. She tucked it in her purse and said, "Next time I'm not wearing panties." She leaned forward and brushed her lips against mine. "We'll see if you can stand it."

I took her to a restaurant in Metairie, a barbecue place that was open twenty-four hours, and watched her devour another big meal. After, I dropped her off a block away from the born again Christian book store.

It was still early by the time I got home. I climbed into bed, but couldn't sleep. Every time I closed my eyes, I saw long legs and blond hair, green eyes and dark pubic hair. I tried thinking of brown velvet eyes, of my old girlfriend's eyes, about the way she used to cry in little gasps when we fucked, her eyes always closed, her mouth open in a little 'O'. She was one great lay. Only problem was, she knew it. A lot of other guys knew it too. Actually, she was more like Xanthe than she would have ever admitted.

#

The next night, I had a call waiting for me at the district station when we knocked off at midnight. It was Xanthe. She was crying. I managed to get what I could out of her and told her not to move. She said she was hurt.

I grabbed Stan on the way out and we beat it downtown to the old hotel that used to be called The Roosevelt, and found Xanthe leaning against the wall in the alley next to the hotel. Her face was bloody and her dress nearly torn off her. She held the dress up as we helped her into the hotel, into a men's room in the lobby.

I stopped her nose bleed and wiped her swollen face as her crying slowly subsided. She pushed my hand away and dampened another towel to wash her own neck. As soon as she took her hands from the front of her black dress, it fell to the floor. She stood there naked under the bright lights of the men's room. I moved over to guard the door while my partner gaped at her.

Finishing, she turned to Stan and asked if he had a comb. "Fuckers stole my purse," she said. There was a nice bruise on her chin and her bottom lip was as swollen as her nose.

"My brush is out in the car," Stan said. "At least your nose ain't broken." He gave her body a good look up and down.

She turned back to the mirror and ran her fingers through her hair and said, "Two fuckin' cowboys decided they weren't gonna pay. So they fucked me. Beat me up and tossed me out of their car."

She looked at herself disgustedly in the mirror and added, "When you sell pussy, someone's bound to come along and take it for nothin'."

"Suppose we go look for them?" Stan said. "I feel like beating the dogshit out of a couple cowboys right about now."

"Your partner looks like the mean type," Xanthe said, turning to Stan and putting a hand on her hip. I could see my partner's eyes roaming down to the thick mat of hair between her legs.

Xanthe turned back to the mirror and said, "Well, I guess I'll give the pussy a break for a couple days." Pointing to her face in the mirror, "Would you pay to fuck this?" Her eyes suddenly teared up.

"Women pay me," Stan said, his eyes examining Xanthe's ass.

That almost caused her to laugh. Bending down, she pulled up her dress and looked at me with eyes that were wet. "You sure look cute in your little uniform," she said as she moved toward me.

I opened the door and let her out first. As soon as I exited, I came face to face with an angry man in a vomit yellow suit. The man's hair was oiled back away from his pudgy face. Posting himself in our way, he said in a loud voice, "What is the meaning of this?"

I pulled Xanthe back and caught Stan moving around me.

"Lighten up, little man," Stan said. The man was actually smaller that me. "As you can see, we're the goddamn police."

The man huffed his chest out and said, "What exactly were you doing in there with that woman?" He folded his tiny arms around his chest.

"Stopping the bleeding," Stan said. "This woman's the victim of a crime, you little weasel-dick."

"Her?" The man with the weasel-dick pointed his chin at Xanthe. "We don't even allow her in this hotel."

"Then how the fuck do you stay in business!" I shouted, jumping around Stan. I stabbed the man in the chest with my forefinger. "You fuck! You get the fuck outta my way before I stick my magnum up your ass and blow your fuckin' brains all over this lobby!"

The little man stumbled back and fell over one of the chairs in the lobby. We left him there. He waited until we were almost out of the door before yelling, "I'm calling you superiors. You can't talk to me like that. You *hit* me!" His little mouth was shaking.

"If I *hit* you, you'd be dead." I yelled back. "Just tell them the boys from the Sixth were here. You *Fuck*!"

On our way to the car, Stan reached over and messed up my hair. I *hate* it when he does that.

"This boy's a regular tiger," he said, "with short people."

"Fuck you!"

Xanthe began to laugh and her nose started bleeding again and didn't stop until we took her over to Charity Hospital for a quick visit to one of the busiest emergency rooms in the world. Stan, who was fucking a couple of the nurses, got Xanthe in and out quickly.

"You see," he said after, "not only do they pay me, but they treat my friends real good."

Only problem was, the moron believed himself.

#

I felt sorry for her. I told Stan and Jack that when we met again, the following evening. Jack wasn't sympathetic.

"It's been around forever," he said. "Whores been beat up as long as they been selling pussy. You can't get stupid over a whore. She might be a good source of information, along with a good source of the clap and syphilis and all kinda diseases that'll rot your dick off like a dried grape.

"I'd like to fuck that little bitch," Stan announced.

Jack blew cigar smoke into Stan's face and said, "Suit yourself."

"She's got a nice, tight little body," Stan explained. "Skinny girls with little tits are mean fucks. She's got a pretty little pussy."

"All pussys are pretty," Jack agreed, "at least from a distance."

The two of them went on a tangent, discussing pussy, describing every imaginable type, from sweet-smelling seventeen-year-olds, to the wide flat ones sported by Bourbon Street strippers. It was a real noteworthy conversation.

"Remember," Stan concluded, elbowing me in the ribs, "a hard-on has no conscience. That bitch strips in front of me again and I'm fuckin' her. I just hope you're there to watch, so I can show you how the big boys do it."

Then the fucker messed up my hair again.

#

I was off the following evening, so I picked up Xanthe and took her to a movie and another late supper. She looked pretty good, despite the bruised chin and swollen lip. Her nose looked fine. With only a hint of lipstick and just enough mascara to make the green in her eyes stand out, Xanthe looked like a regular girl on a regular date. She'd worn a man's dress white shirt with her blue jeans. We saw *Close Encounters Of The Third Kind* at a theater in Metairie. Her only reaction after was, "I wonder how much those little guys would charge for a head job?" Then she winked at me.

It was over dinner, over a deep bowl of crawfish bisque, that she slipped me the news.

"The spick's called Cool Rat. He stays in a house on Mazant Street, a couple blocks from the Desire Projects." She had nice skin, pearly white, too nice for a whore. "He's a little guy with black hair and a big brown birthmark on the side of his face." She pointed to the right side of her jaw. "He supposed to be bad."

I put my fork down.

"Can you believe I got laid, looking like this? The guy who knows the spick upped with the info."

She took a sip of tea. "I don't know the nigger's name yet, but I'm fuckin' Cool Rat tomorrow night, so I'll just fuck the name outta him."

"No way," I said. "Don't do that."

"Why not?"

"Don't meet him. Don't go near him. I'll pass the information to Homicide."

"But, why?"

"It's too dangerous."

She laughed in my face. "Don't be a whiny baby," she said.

She became quiet after that, and so did I. I was having problems with this, sending her into the wolf's lair with only her pussy. It was then, in the silence, that I saw something in her eyes that made me feel like shit. I saw a longing in those green eyes, a desire, a needing that needed to be filled, a needing I could not fill. I could make love to her all right. But I knew, deep down, that I could never satisfy, could never match the caring I saw in those eyes as she looked back at me across the table.

Sometimes, I can feel the Sicilian in me, like a virus. I can feel a wave of ruthless Sicilian blood rush through my veins, and find myself doing things that I thought only a Mafioso could do. I felt my heart growing stone cold as I sat across from her.

"Could you hold me a while?" Xanthe asked later, as we pulled up in front of the born again Christian book store. I followed her hips upstairs and lay next to her on the mattress. I even wrapped my arms around her and listened to her breathing. Heavy at first, her breathing eased into steady breaths as she snuggled with me. As soon as she fell asleep, I left.

I tacked a note on the inside of her door, telling her to stay away from Cool Rat, but I knew she wouldn't listen. Deep down I knew.

The next time I saw her, she was propped up in that fuckin' streetcar.

It was my fault. As soon as I told Stan about Cool Rat, the next evening at roll call, he told me what would happen. When I got off, I changed out of my uniform and hurried to Xanthe's but she wasn't there. She wasn't there the following morning either. Nor the next day.

Fuck if Stan wasn't right. On that hot, muggy night, we both watched Xanthe the blond hauled away, like so much dead meat.

#

It took the Homicide Division less that three hours to secure a warrant for the arrest of Jose Luis Garcia, also known as Cool Rat, also known as Jose Obisbo, also known as The Knifer, for the murder of Thelma Wortling, also known as Xanthe. They found his fingerprints in the streetcar, matched it with my sworn statement and took it to a judge.

On that same hot, sticky night, Homicide Sergeant Rob Mason led a group of officers, including Jack, Stan and me, to a house on Mazant Street. Two homicide men spotted Cool Rat return home alone an hour earlier. Mason, a lean man with a square jaw and a Marine Corps haircut, was the man in charge of my brother's murder case. He looked tired that morning when he gave us last minute instructions before we arrived on Mazant. He made everyone don a bullet proof vest. Since it was Mason's warrant, he would be the first man in.

Cool Rat lived in a small, wooden house on the downtown side of Mazant, exactly three blocks from the projects. Mason let Stan kick in the front door, after we'd surrounded the place. At exactly four o'clock in the morning, Stan kicked and Mason went in first, followed by two more homicide men. Jack and I scrambled in behind them. Stan remained by the door, to guard our rear. He didn't like it one bit, but no one was up to arguing with Mason.

Once inside the dark house that smelled of sweaty blankets and refried beans, Mason moved to the left with one of his men. Jack and I followed the other homicide man into a bedroom on the right. There was a lamp on in the room, next to an unmade bed.

In movies, it happened in slow motion. In real life, it happened at a hundred miles an hour. Fanning out in the small room, I stepped over to the bed and touched it. It was warm and tacky wet. I wiped my hand on the side of my jeans and moved to the door of a walk-in closet. I could feel my heart thundering in my throat as I threw open the closet door. Nothing but clothes.

The homicide man, who opened the other closet door, didn't have a chance. I saw it happen. I saw the blur of an arm and the silver blade of a butcher knife slash down, catching the homicide man in the face, sending him back on top of me. I heard a scream and saw a maniacal dark face descend on us, saw the knife rise again.

A gun roared and roared again and again. Cool Rat twitched as the bullets struck. Blood spurted from his neck, all over me. He fell to one side and tumbled to the floor, across my feet. I felt myself shoving the detective off of me and pulling myself away from Cool Rat.

The detective was bleeding profusely from his face. Jack pulled him away and shoved a rag against the cut. Mason took over and pulled his man to the doorway and began working on him.

"Get an ambulance!" Mason yelled.

"You OK?" Jack had me by the arm and twisted me around.

"Yeah," I told him and I stumbled back on the bed and wiped the blood from my neck and arms. Jack took a step toward the closet and Cool Rat rose up at him, the knife still in his hand. Jack pumped three more shots into the face of the bastard.

"*You motha' fucka!*" Jack screamed. He reached over, snatched my magnum from my hand and emptied it in Cool Rat's head. Six rounds of semi-jacketed hollow points slapped the head around viciously.

Then Jack stepped back, his face contorted in a hideous grimace. Glaring at the body, he handed me my gun and said, "Fucker's dead now!"

I remember Stan stumbling in at that point, pissed off as hell, yelling, "Fuck. I'm *always* in the wrong place!"

#

The homicide detective would live with a scar that would mar his face forever. Jose Luis Garcia, alias Cool Rat, alias Jose Obisbo, alias The Knifer, was buried in St. Louis Cemetery Number Three with full Catholic honors, the fucker! Sergeant Rob

Mason was suspended for allowing Jack Blanc, Stan Smith and Dino LaStanza to go on the warrant. We had to talk Jack out of paying a visit to the funeral parlor. We told him, he'd already gotten his man — twice.

"Now," he added, "one day, we'll get the nigger, too."

"Fuckin Ay!" Stan said.

I said nothing.

The newspaper crucified us, labeling us as 'killer cops', questioning our late night tactics. They went ballistic as soon as they matched my name with my brother's. It was a vendetta, plain and simple. Even if I hadn't fired a shot, bullets from *my* weapon were found in Cool Rat's brain. But even as a rookie, I knew better than pay attention to the newspapers. Fuck 'em!

#

Xanthe's mother arrived at New Orleans International Airport on a bright spring morning, to claim her only daughter's body. I met her and took her to the funeral parlor where her daughter waited in a pine casket. Mrs. Wortling was a gray haired woman with hunched shoulders and lifeless gray eyes. She didn't say a word to me as I drove her to the parlor and back to the airport, behind the hearse.

There was a little time before her flight back to Jackson, so I asked Mrs. Wortling if she would like some coffee. She nodded slightly and followed me to the restaurant that looked out on the runways. After we sat, I handed Mrs. Wortling a recent picture of Xanthe. It was a mug shot that I had the crime lab blow up and cut off the numbers. I guess it still looked like a mug shot. Mrs. Wortling began to cry softly, as she looked at the image of her dead daughter.

She never touched her coffee. I could barely stomach my own coffee, sitting there with guilt hanging around my neck like a fuckin' albatross the size of a jumbo jet.

"Mrs. Wortling," I said, when she finally stopped crying. "I've got to tell you something."

She looked up at me.

"Those things the papers said about . . . Thelma . . . weren't true." On the front page of the paper they'd printed a full mug shot of Xanthe, next to a mug shot of Cool Rat, detailing their deaths. Beneath Xanthe's picture was the word, 'prostitute'.

"Thelma was helping us," I told her. "She was helping the police. She wasn't what the papers said about her. Not at all. She was special. She was my — friend."

My words had no effect. They only caused my throat to tighten. I never felt so useless. When her flight was announced, I walked Mrs. Wortling to the gate. She actually started walking faster the closer we got to the gate. She couldn't wait to get out of New Orleans. And she never looked back.

#

It wasn't long after the Desire Streetcar Murder that the city announced it would renovate the dilapidated U.S. Mint that stands at the end of the French Market. Plans were approved to brighten up that entire dark corner of the French Quarter. They planned to move the Desire Streetcar into the courtyard of the Mint, and make a decent monument out of it.

But when I think about it, I wish I never heard of the streetcar named Desire.

A Heartbeat

Joseph LaStanza bought it on a rainy morning, at 2:07 a.m. exactly, while answering a burglary-in-progress call at a warehouse at the corner of St. Claude and Elysian Fields Avenue. He never saw it coming. Holstering his PR24 nightstick as he stepped from his marked unit, he never felt it. The next second he lay face down on the cement, a bullet in the back of his head.

He felt himself rise from the body and drift straight up. He saw his body lying in the gutter, a pool of blood collecting around his head. Drifting into the starless sky, through the rain, he looked down at the dark rooftops of New Orleans as they slowly faded. He slipped into a blackness so complete he felt nothing, saw nothing, heard nothing. After a while, a long while, he thought he heard something faintly in the distance.

He strained to hear. The sound gradually grew closer until he recognized it as a clatter, a rhythmic clatter that became louder and louder. A sharp whistle blew and his eyes snapped open. His face was pressed against glass. He blinked and looked out a window at a snowy field passing outside. Joe pulled his cheek from the window pane and looked around.

The coach was well lit and empty; and the train seemed to be in a big hurry, rattling over the rails, snowy fields rolling past outside. There were distant hills looming in the darkness. The coach shivered over the rails, rocking slightly from side to side.

Joe looked at his reflection in the window. He ran his right hand over the back of his head and found no wound there. He looked down at his sky-blue N.O.P.D. uniform shirt, ran his left hand over his gold star-and-crescent badge, down to his holster to the black rubber grip of his stainless steel .357 magnum Smith and Wesson. It felt solid and real.

He checked the nearest door. It was locked. Wiping his hands on his pants, he reached for the door handle again. It didn't feel right. It felt soft. No, his fingers were getting numb. He went and checked the other door. It was locked. So were the windows.

He looked at his reflection in the window again and saw something else. Like in a movie, he saw his lieutenant standing behind the roll-call podium, a black wreath hung from the front of the podium. His lieutenant spoke.

". . . killed in the line of duty summary." His lieutenant struggled to keep his voice steady. "As some of you already know, early this morning Sergeant Joseph LaStanza was shot to death at the corner of St. Claude and Elysian Fields . . ."

Joe blinked and saw his mother sitting in a funeral parlor. Her face taut, her hair tied in a bun, she sat stiffly at the edge of a sofa as many people dressed in black moved around her. Her eyes were vacant and hollow.

His father stood next to a coffin, his head bent over, his shoulders moving up and down as he wept over the coffin. A figure moved up next to him and put a hand on the old man's shoulder. The figure turned and Joe saw it was his younger brother. Dino's face was drawn and pale, his eyes damp and red.

The view changed. It slipped away, like a movie camera on a gurney rolling away from the scene. Joe reached out and touched the window. Through his numbing fingers it felt smooth, but not cold. It should be cold with the snow outside.

The door opened behind him. He waited a second before turning. A young woman stood just inside the doorway. Smallish, a couple inches above five feet, the girl had long dark brown hair and gold-brown eyes and was very pretty. She looked to be about twenty. In a yellow sun-dress, with bare shoulders, and white sandals, she should be shivering, only she wasn't.

The girl looked down at herself and ran her hands down the front of her body. She turned and looked past Joe as if she didn't see him, blinked her wide eyes and pursed her full lips.

When he stood, she jumped and her mouth opened into a wide 'O'.

"Who?" Her lips quivered. "Who are you?" Her hands reached out to steady herself as the train passed over rougher tracks.

"Where am I?"

Joe shook his head and shrugged.

The girl fell into the nearest seat. "I was walking home," she said. Her wide brown eyes looked glazed. She blinked at Joe. "He hurt me."

She turned away and looked out the window. Joe looked back at the window and saw a long beach and turquoise water streaked in purple and green. The picture moved and he saw a girl lying on the beach. In a dark blue bikini, the girl lay on her belly, her long brown hair spread around her neck.

A man lay on the other side of the girl. The man sat up suddenly and picked up a bottle of suntan lotion. Joe collapsed into a seat. It was *Dino*, Joe's little brother.

Dino knelt next to the girl and poured dark liquid on her back and rubbed it into her skin. The girl moved her head and looked at Dino and smiled. Joe craned his neck forward for a closer look. He looked back at the girl in the sundress and then back at the girl in the bikini. It was the same girl.

He stood and moved to the seat in front of her and saw tears on her face.

She blinked at him again.

"Is that you?"

She shook her head and put a hand over her mouth. "My twin."

Joe looked back at the window. The scene had changed. Dino and the girl were slow dancing in an open-air cabana bar, banana trees swayed outside. Dino wore a blue and green island shirt and white pants. The girl wore a red sarong. Joe could see the ocean beyond, rolling to shore as the sun set. Dino pulled away from the girl and then leaned forward to kiss her on the lips. She closed her eyes and turned her head and opened her mouth and kissed him back a long time. Joe blinked and the scene changed.

Dino and the girl sat eating at a long table, a large glass chandelier suspended above them. They ate quietly. It looked like grillades and grits. Joe noticed the wedding ring on the girl's ring finger.

The train rocked. The girl stood, catching Joe's attention. She wiped the tears from her cheeks as she stared at the window. "That's my house."

Joe cleared his throat. "That's my brother."

The girl looked at him and narrowed her eyes.

"My little brother and your sister. Looks like they're married."

Joe turned back to the scene and watched Dino pick up his plate. His wife picked hers up and followed him into a bright kitchen.

"His name's Dino."

"Lizette. Her name's Lizette."

The girl's eyes were wide again. "Where are we?"

"I don't know. Exactly. I remember stepping out of my police car and that's all."

The girl's chin sank to her chest. "I remember . . ." She shuddered and wrapped her arms around herself. "I was walking home. I saw a shadow move. A man." Closing her eyes, she began to shake. "It burned. It hurt. I felt my blood on my arms and back. He . . . he had a knife!"

She screamed. Joe jumped up and grabbed her arms, but pulled his hands away fast. She caught her breath and looked down at her arms. Joe looked at his hands and rubbed his fingers. They were even more numb now.

Joe sat back down and closed his eyes and remembered, of all things, how he and Dino used to play hide-and-seek in St. Patrick's Cemetery and Odd Fellow's Rest at night, hunting make-believe vampires with wooden stakes, creeping between the crypts, hiding behind the sepulchres, scaring the daylights out of each other back when their world one big playground.

He felt sad, very sad. He felt a well of emotion in his throat and opened his eyes. His face was wet. He wiped it.

The girl cleared her throat behind him. "They look happy."

Joe looked back at the window and saw Dino and Lizette sitting on a couch watching TV. Snuggled in each other's arms, they looked as natural as anything he'd ever seen.

The girl let out a faint half-laugh. "Looks like my little sister found her soulmate."

"What?"

"My sister always believed there was someone perfect for everyone. A perfect soulmate for everyone. The hard part was to find that person." The girl blinked and stuck her chin out. "I never found mine." Her voice was deeper now and thick with emotion.

She turned her gold-brown eyes toward Joe and said, "Did you find yours?"

He thought of his ex-wife. No way she was his soulmate. He shook his head.

"I was married once," he said. "I don't know about soulmates."

"If you found her, you'd know." The girl looked away. "I never found mine." Her chin sank to her chest. "Maybe my sister has found hers. I hope so."

Joe thought about his ex. They were so different. They were never passionate. They were just not that much in love, if that was what it meant. It made him feel even sadder.

He looked around the coach, at the clean seats, at the pristine windows and felt so alone. He closed his eyes and thought about his mother's face, about her smile, about spaghetti dinners in a house that was warm and comfortable. He remembered his father's beard hot against his face when he hugged the old man, remembered long summer nights sharing a bed with his little brother, dreaming about what he would be when he grew up.

He wanted to be a space man. To ride the stars. He grew up to be a blue knight, like his father. Only there was no suit of armor, no round table, no Camelot. Joe opened his eyes and looked down at his blue shirt and knew it wasn't enough.

He opened his mouth to tell the girl, but the train braked. He grabbed the back of the seat in front of him as he leaned forward then back as the train stopped.

The door opened behind them.

The girl stood up. She looked around in genuine fear.

"I don't want to go," she said, her lower lip quivering.

Joe felt himself rise. He tried to fight it, but couldn't.

The girl moved to the open door. She reached back for him. When he reached for her she was gone.

He felt himself being pulled toward the same door. He tried to grab one of the seats, but couldn't get a grip. He tried holding on to the doorway, but when he reached for it, it was gone. He moved into darkness. He moved into blackness so black he could not feel his breath, could not feel anything. In the distance, he heard a faint sound. He felt a warmth all around. The sound grew louder and louder until he recognized it.

It was a heartbeat.

This story is for debb

The Man With Moon Hands

Before the meat wagon arrived, LaStanza went to take a look at the body. He didn't need a flashlight. The bright moon shined directly into that dirty New Orleans alley. Just inside the alley, LaStanza passed a young patrolman with sandy hair explaining to the other policemen, "He had a gun."

The body was about half way down the dead end alley. LaStanza's partner, Paul Snowood, stood over it. Next to him, a crime lab technician was reloading his camera.

"Come see this," Snowood twanged. "Got him through the pump with one shot." In his cowboy hat, rope tie around the neck of his western shirt, brown jeans and snakeskin boots, Detective Snowood couldn't look more out of place if he tried.

"You sure you don't want me to take this?" LaStanza asked as he stepped up.

"You're up to your ass in murders already, boy, " Snowood said. "This ain't nothin' but paperwork." Tilting his Stetson back, Snowood pointed to the body with his note pad and added, "Anyway, it looks like a good shootin'."

The body was on its side, legs straight out, arms contorted like soft pretzels. There were holes in the soles of both shoes and a worn spot on the man's jeans above the left knee. A stain of dark blood had gathered beneath the twisted torso. A small caliber, blue steel semi-automatic lay two feet from the man's head. It was a typical Saturday-night-special.

"You can handle the canvass for me, if you've a hankerin'."

"Sure," LaStanza said as he leaned over the body.

It was a white male, mid-twenties, about five feet - eight inches tall, one hundred and eighty pounds with frizzy brown hair and a large gunshot wound in the center of his chest. Stepping out of the way of the technician, LaStanza paused and looked back at the body. There was something familiar about it. That was when he saw the hands.

He found some empty soft drink cases a few feet away and sat on them as his partner and the technician began taking measurements. Tugging angrily on his moustache, LaStanza stared at the pallid hands, at the limp fingers that looked like white goldfish left out to rot, and remembered . . .

#

LaStanza had been riding alone that night when the call came out.

"Headquarters — any Sixth District Unit. Signal 103M with a gun. 2300 block of Rousseau."

A disturbance on Rousseau Street involving a mental case with a gun. There was only one appropriate thought: "Fuck Me!"

It was a typically busy night in the Bloody Sixth District. LaStanza was the only one available. He flipped on his blue lights, accelerated and made it to Rousseau in less than two minutes. He found a small gathering in the 2300 block, about a dozen people standing in the street in front of an alley between a large warehouse and a junk yard. He was surprised to see a white face in the crowd.

As he climbed out, the white face approached and pointed to the alley and said, "My son's in there with a twenty-five automatic. He's a mental patient." The man was tall and very thin and wore thick spectacles.

"What's his problem?" LaStanza asked the spectacles.

"He's crazy."

"Who gave him the gun?"

"I did. I mean it's mine."

Crazy? It ran in the family. Now it was LaStanza's problem. There was a loony-tune in an alley with a gun. LaStanza withdrew his stainless steel .357 Smith and Wesson and approached the alley. He could see the young man clearly, standing under a light near the side door of the warehouse.

The man paid no attention to LaStanza moving into the alley. Looking up at the sky, the loony-tune ran his left hand through his frizzy hair. In his right hand he held a small, blue steel automatic. He looked to be in his early twenties.

When he finally noticed LaStanza, he craned his neck forward and grinned. His large, bulbous eyes batted frantically at the approaching patrolman. He slowly raised the automatic, pointed it toward LaStanza, who ducked into the shadows.

The man went, "Zap. Zap." He followed this with a frightened laugh. His hand was shaking so hard, LaStanza thought the gun would fall.

The .357 magnum was cocked and pointed center on the man's chest.

"Put it down," LaStanza told the man as calmly as he could, "or I'll blow your brains out the back of your head." LaStanza's hands were steady, his voice flat and dry.

Then man laughed again as his gun slowly inched forward until he let it drop to the ground. Then he raised his hands and said, "You see these hands?" The man glared at the huge white digits at the end of his palms. "They're not my hands. They're moon hands!"

LaStanza moved forward, stepped on the automatic, holstered his magnum and slapped a handcuff across the loony's right wrist.

"These aren't my hands," the man complained as he tried to put his free hand in front of LaStanza's eyes. With a quick jerk, LaStanza twisted the man around and cuffed both hands him behind his back before picking up the automatic.

"They're *moon* hands!" the man cried.

On the way to Charity Hospital, the man told LaStanza he was a second generation clone. Then he started pleading for the LaStanza to take him to Tchoupitoulas and Jackson Avenue – to catch his flight – to Alpha Six.

"This one needs a ride," LaStanza told the standard-issue, heavy-set, flat-faced admitting nurse. "Put him on the nonstop to Mandeville." It was nut house time, absolutely.

"Must be a full moon tonight," the bored nurse said. "All the loonies are out."

While LaStanza was filling out his report, a Seventh District patrolman came in with a howling man.

"What's his problem?" LaStanza asked.

"He thinks the world's being taken over by clones."

LaStanza couldn't resist. "Put him in with mine. He's a second generation clone."

The patrolman eagerly obliged. LaStanza and the other cop watched the two men standing at opposite ends of the small trauma room, hissing and spitting at one another. LaStanza laughed so hard, his side ached. He'd been on the street long enough to not pass up an opportunity like that. Laughs were hard to find along the bloody streets of the Sixth District.

The Man With Moon Hands became one of LaStanza's favorite cop stories, especially after the man was released, as all nut cases inevitably were. The frizzy-haired loony began waiting every night at Tchoupitoulas and Jackson Avenue – for his flight – to Alpha Six. No matter the weather, he would be there, standing with his tattered brown suitcase in front of the old, abandoned New Orleans Cotton Exchange. No one bothered him. Most people probably figured he was just waiting in the wrong place for the Jackson Avenue Ferry.

One evening LaStanza watched The Man With Moon Hands for an hour and the man never moved a muscle. He stood patiently, the moon hands wrapped around the suitcase, the bulging eyes tilted upward at the dark sky, as he waited – for his flight – to Alpha Six.

Then LaStanza got transferred to Homicide. Three years later, LaStanza was in a different alley.

#

"What's the matter wit' you?" Snowood yelled, "I thought you was gonna canvass?"

LaStanza climbed off the cases and started down the alley. He was still looking at the body.

"Mark and I are taking Wyatt, Jr. here to the Bureau for his statement," Snowood said. To Snowood, a cop who shot someone had to be related, no matter how distantly, to Wyatt Earp, himself.

LaStanza watched as the corpse was zipped into a black body bag and hauled off by the coroner's assistants. In the span of two minutes, he was alone. But there was nothing to canvass. It was a dead end alley with no doors or windows, just brick walls and rusted dumpsters and bent-up garbage cans. It was a garbage alley.

It became very quiet. If he strained, LaStanza could hear cars in the distance, but it was silent in the alley. There was no movement except for the gnats circling over the fresh blood, and the rats crouching in anticipation of the moment when the detective would be gone.

On his way out of the alley, he remembered something else. He remembered yet another alley, back when he was a rookie. It was Mardi Gras morning and someone had killed a cop. LaStanza found the cop killer in a foggy alley. The man had a gun and it was over in less than a second. It was a good shooting, a clean shooting.

He'd shot the man without hesitation. And he wondered about that, about the intangible, about the unspoken reason a cop shoots one and not another. Maybe there was something in the moon man's frantic eyes that told LaStanza not to shoot. Maybe it was the frizzy hair. Or maybe, it was the moon white hands.

#

"Looks like a good shooting," Sergeant Mark Land told LaStanza when he arrived at the Homicide Office. "Looks like our man had no choice."

LaStanza sat heavily in his chair and didn't answer.

Big, burly and Italian, with thick dark hair and a full moustache, Mark looked like an oversized version of LaStanza.

Grinning broadly, the sergeant pulled up Snowood's chair and began to run down the patrolman's statement in detail, but LaStanza wasn't listening. He was thinking about the faded bricks of the old Cotton Exchange and the rusted drain pipes and all the lonely nights spent looking up at an empty sky.

When Mark finished, he yawned and said, "Shit, we'll be outta here in no time."

LaStanza leaned back in his chair and closed his eyes, but only for a moment.

"Say boy, what's wrong wit' you?" Snowood called out as he approached. "You been acting spooky."

"It's nothing."

"Don't give me that shit. What's the matter?"

"Nothing, I told you." LaStanza scooped up his black coffee mug with its small inscription that read: FUCK THIS SHIT! He moved over to the coffee pot and poured the hot coffee-and-chicory into his mug, then filled his sergeant's cup when Mark stepped up. The young patrolman moved up with a Styrofoam cup. LaStanza put the pot down and turned away.

"Something wrong?" the patrolman quickly asked in a shaky voice.

"No," Mark answered quickly.

LaStanza turned back and looked at the patrolman, noticing how the man's hand shook when he poured the coffee.

"He pulled the same gun on me a couple years ago," LaStanza said.

"What?" Mark said as he nearly spilled his coffee.

LaStanza took in a deep breath before adding, "That was The Man With Moon Hands."

"I'll be damned!" Mark did spill his coffee this time. Switching his cup to his other hand, Mark turned to the patrolman and said, "You killed a legend tonight, pal."

"What are y'all yakkin' about?" Snowood asked from his desk.

"Your victim was The Man With Moon Hands," Mark told him.

"No shit?"

LaStanza watched the patrolman's eyes. There was confusion in the eyes, along with a touch of fear.

"You never heard of The Man With Moon Hands?" Mark asked the patrolman.

"No," the man answered softly. "I've only been on the road six months."

"He was the most famous 103M in the city."

"At least we know who he is now," Snowood injected. "Sumbitch had no ID on him."

"He was a 103M?" the patrolman asked LaStanza, who did not respond. Turning back at Mark, the patrolman added, "He did look weird."

"What was his name?" Snowood asked his partner.

"I don't remember," LaStanza answered, still watching the patrolman, "but it's gotta be in the computer."

"Well I'll be," the patrolman sighed in relief. "He was crazy!"

LaStanza couldn't stop his voice from sounding vicious, "You couldn't see that?"

"What am I?" the patrolman snapped back, "a psychiatrist?" He seemed stunned.

LaStanza gave him the Sicilian stare, the one that went straight through to the back of the man's skull. Then he walked back to his desk and flopped in his chair.

The exasperated patrolman continued explaining to Mark, "He looked right at me and pointed the gun and zapped me." The patrolman's voice began to rise as he followed the sergeant back into the interview room. "How'd he get the gun back anyway?"

"Goddamn courts release everything now days," Mark growled angrily.

#

LaStanza was finishing his daily report, when the patrolman approached. Snowood had gone to the computer to try and identify The Man With Moon Hands.

"Excuse me, Detective LaStanza. Can I have a word with you?" The patrolman looked like a dog lost out in the rain.

LaStanza nodded to his partner's empty chair.

The patrolman's voice was almost a whisper, "I didn't know he was . . . a legend."

"He was a second generation clone."

"What?"

"Forget it."

The patrolman's hands were shaking again. He looked like he wanted to run away. Gulping, he managed to say, "How was I supposed to know?"

LaStanza said nothing.

"He pointed a gun at me."

"You didn't see a tall man with thick glasses near the alley, did you?"

"No." The patrolman looked back anxiously.

LaStanza just nodded and went back to his daily.

After a minute, the whisper voice of the patrolman came back. "When he drew down on you, why didn't you shoot him?"

There it was again, the intangible. How do you explain what couldn't be explained? How do you explain what was incapable of even being comprehended by the mind, incapable of being distinguished by any of the senses? How do you explain something like that?

LaStanza knew he could not. You just knew.

Peering back into a pair of searching eyes, LaStanza recognized something. He recognized a look. It was a look that said, "I've got something to live with for the rest of my life." He'd seen that same look in his own mirror.

"I passed the shoot-don't-shoot class with an 'A' at the academy," the patrolman said in a strained voice.

"Some things can't be taught," LaStanza said, finally. "Some things can't even be explained. You just know."

"You didn't shoot him and I did," the patrolman said. "Why?"

"I just knew."

It was as if he'd reached over and slapped the patrolman across the face. It took a second for the man to recover. He looked away from LaStanza's eyes and took in a couple breaths before asking, "Do you think I'll have any trouble with the Grand Jury?"

"Don't worry about it," LaStanza heard himself say. "It was a good shooting."

This story is for Josie

Bet the Devil

Every fiction should have a moral;
and, what is more the purpose, the critics
have discovered that every fiction *has*.
Never Bet the Devil Your Head

by Edgar
Allan Poe

This morning, on my fortieth birthday, I drove to St. Bernard Parish and bought some rat poison so I could boil it down for the arsenic residue to put in that rat bastard Coleman Hay's coffee.

I boiled it in a big black pot, the whole box of poison. It stunk so badly I had to open all the windows. It took almost two hours and the damn residue was no good. I put it in some coffee, but it smelled so strong I knew it wouldn't work. So I threw it away, pot and all, out over the back fence in the empty lot. Maybe a rat'll eat it.

That goon Riley upstairs watched me, his little pink face peeking at me through the window screen. I shot him the bird on my way back in; and he jumped away from the screen, the little weasel.

I turned up the AC and took a shower, but it was no use. As soon as I got out the oil seeped back into my hair and it was greasy even before I dried it. I locked up my apartment and got back into my Datsun — that's right, they were still *Datsuns* when my heap was put together back in '72. It's an eye-catcher now sporting three colors, if you count rust as a color.

I drove the wrong way down Piety Street to Chartres to go back to St. Bernard to buy a gun. I like going the wrong way down one-way streets in New Orleans because there are too many damn one-way streets. Hell, we're the *only* city on earth where you can find three one-ways in a row, all going the same way. If you want to go the other way — hell, what's the use in arguing. I just go the way I want.

It took me a good half hour to make it back to the parish and another fifteen minutes before I pulled up in front of the St. Bernard Gun and Jewelry Shop. A guy with an orange crew-cut and an NRA tee-shirt told me I was a lucky guy. A week from now the Brady law goes into effect and I'd have to wait five days to get my gun.

Lucky for me, and unlucky for Coleman Hay, I walked out of the St. Bernard Gun and Jewelry Shop with a blue steel Smith & Wesson Model 15 Combat Masterpiece .38 caliber revolver. Snub-nosed with a two-inch barrel, I could carry it in my pocket. I bought a box of .38 'plus P' ammunition. I think the guy said 'plus P' meant plus power. Driving back into the city, I slipped six rounds into the cylinder. The checkered walnut stock felt so warm in my hand.

I caught the pain-in-the-ass St. Claude Avenue bridge, and was about to climb out of my car and put a couple slugs into the head of that goddamn bridge operator when a New Orleans police car pulled up behind me. So I just waited for twenty sweaty goddamn minutes for two ratty-looking tugs to chug through the locks from the river.

Closing my eyes, I could just see Coleman Hay's prissy face as I walk into his office and pull out the gun and point it between his beady eyes. His eyes grow wide. I squeeze the trigger until his head splits open like a melon. Then I put the gun down and wait for the cops and the media.

I could see the headlines — Playwright Slays Director of Downtown Arts Center. Beneath my picture would be the caption, "Yogi Bolds, whose plays were repeatedly rejected by the slain director, took out his revenge with a Smith & Wesson."

Sure, I'd spend some time in jail. I could use the time to write more plays, probably become the editor of that prison newspaper, the one touted on CNN. People won't forget my name. And one day I'll get out and Coleman Hay will still be dead.

A tap on the horn behind me brought me back to the bridge and the heat. I made sure I didn't break any traffic laws until after the cop car turned off on Desire Street. I made an illegal left turn at Franklin Avenue, just to piss off the other drivers, and took Chartres back to Piety Street.

I was in no special hurry. Coleman Hay never breezed into work until after 'doing' lunch with an uptown snob or two. So I sat on my sofa, unloaded my Combat Masterpiece — God, what a great name for a gun — and dry-fired it. The slap of the hammer sounded nice and solid as it fell. I aimed it at the TV and it went click. I aimed it at the AC unit chugging in the window and it went click. I closed my eyes and aimed it between Coleman Hay's eyes and it went click.

Putting the Combat Masterpiece down, I went into my kitchen and pulled out the originals of my plays, all four of them, out of the refrigerator. Pulling them out of the extra-thick cardboard box, I laid them out on my bed so the cops would find them easily.

Then I went into my closet and pulled down the Xerox copies of my plays.

I found my phone book under the kitchen sink.

I found four unused envelopes, each big enough for a copy of each play, grabbed a red Bic pen and sat at my kitchen table. I addressed the envelopes to each of the TV stations and one to the newspapers. Then I wrote four copies of the same note to put in each envelope. It said, "Coleman Hay died because he was too stupid to stage these plays!"

The kitchen clock read eleven o'clock.

I went back out to my sofa, sat down and closed my eyes and thought about my plays. Sweat rolled down my temples. I let it.

I pretended that I was being interviewed about killing Coleman Hay. That pretty blonde reporter from Channel 4 held a microphone in front of my face. So did that tall, skinny black guy from Channel 6 *and* that pretty black reporter from Channel 8, the one with the one long eye-brow across her forehead. I was handcuffed, but I could talk.

"Coleman Hay sent my first play back, saying he didn't find anything special in *The Huge, Sensitive German.* He actually said he didn't think a story about an ex-Nazi would capture an audience. Yeah? Well *Schindler's List* won the goddamn Academy Award!

"OK, so Schindler wasn't in the SS like my hero, but he was a party member. OK, so Schindler saved a lot of people. *My* hero ended up disliking Hitler.

"Coleman Hay was even more brutal in rejecting my second play. He didn't even like the title, *Masticating Decatur Street.*

"What else could I name a story about a prostitute and a street cleaner?"

The pretty reporter with the long eye-brow would nod in agreement.

"He sent a form rejection slip when he rejected my third play, *Chartreuse Azaleas.* He didn't like the title either. *Steel Magnolias* — now that's a good title, but not *my* title.

"But the topper was my last play. He kept it six months before sending it back. How many times did I sit across the street from the Downtown Arts Center, on that broken concrete bench and dream about opening night?

"For the record, Coleman Hay rejected *Uptown Women in Beige con Mandingos,* a breakthrough play about race relations, for a piece of tripe called *Slimy Things Did Crawl With Legs Upon The Slimy Sea* written by a goddamn university professor. So what if it's a line from Coleridge, it's a dumb title!"

My play clearly showed the guilt uptown white women feel toward black men because of slavery. The slimy play was *science-fiction.*

I looked at the clock. It was eleven-fifteen.

I got up and peeled off my shirt. I threw it against the wall and it stuck, it was so soaked. It slid down a moment later, leaving

113

a wet mark on the wall and it occurred to me that I'll probably
leave a red stain on Coleman Hay's pretty wallpaper.

I went in the bathroom and climbed out of my shorts and
turned on the shower, then thought — what if the gun doesn't
work? What if I pull it out, point it between those evil eyes, pull
the trigger and it *doesn't* fire?

I hurried back into the front room, reloaded the Combat
Masterpiece and brought it back to my bedroom. I grabbed my
pillow, shoved it against the gun's muzzle and pointed the gun at
my mattress. I squeezed the trigger until the gun fired. It was
louder than I thought and kicked more than I thought.

My ears rang. The room smelled of burnt gunpowder and
burned pillow. I put the gun on the bed next to my stories and took
the pillow into the bathroom. I ran it under the faucet to put it out.
It smoked pretty good.

Then I took my shower and put on a new Army-surplus
green tee-shirt, brown jeans and my green and brown canvass
authentic Vietnam jungle combat boots. The oil was back in my
hair already, but I didn't give a damn.

I got six fresh cartridges and reloaded the Combat
Masterpiece. I slipped it into the waistband of my jeans at the
small of my back. Then I filled my pockets with the rest of the
bullets and put on my favorite Khaki shirt to wear out over my tee-
shirt to hide the gun. On my way out I grabbed my Cleveland
Indians baseball cap and pulled it on my head.

I went the right way up Piety Street to Royal Street and
took my time going through the Quarter, looking at the multi-
colored buildings and the black balconies and the painted women
and overweight men wearing the wrong colors. Finally leaving the
Quarter, I drove through the central business district and into the
warehouse district, thinking this city has too many goddamn
districts.

At exactly one o'clock I parked my car next to a meter at
the corner of Poeyfarre and Constance Street, climbed out and
stretched. I reached around to adjust the gun in my waistband and

it felt wet. I was soaked with sweat and nervous as hell, but I was happy.

I walked around to the side of the Downtown Arts Center and spotted Coleman Hay's white Mercedes parked in its reserved parking spot. I went back around to the front of the old red brick building and went in the front door. I took the elevator up to the reception area and breezed passed the receptionist who was too busy yakking on the phone to even look up.

Coleman Hay's pretty blonde private secretary pulled her tight yellow skirt down, like she always does when I come in, crossed her legs and asked if I had an appointment.

"Not today," I said in a low, mousy voice. Looking down, all humble and all, I said, "I was hoping I could talk to Mr. Hay for a minute, if it's not too much to ask." Backing away from her desk, I pointed to one of the waiting chairs. "I'll just sit here, if you don't mind."

"Suit yourself," she said. "It's going to be a while. Mr. Coleman has a full slate."

"I'll wait."

She snapped her gum at me and went back to filing her nails. She never looked me in the eye, ever. She always wore tight skirts and always looked just past me when she had to talk to me.

I'd planned to just walk past her, right into Coleman's office, but just as I'd walked up to her desk I thought, "What if he's not in there? What if he's down the hall? What if he's in the men's room?"

I wiped the sweat from my face and sat as still as I could. I closed my eyes and thought about — *Uptown Women in Beige con Mandingos*. I could see Muffy Rosenberg-St. Cyr standing on the rear deck of her uptown home. Watching the tall, black gardener who is shirtless as he cuts her grass, her mouth trembles as she exclaims, "The guilt. The guilt. The guilt!"

Facing the gardener, Muffy unbuttons her blouse and pulls off her brassiere to expose her breasts to the gardener and says, "I can no longer live with the guilt in my breast. Look at me. Look, as I stand half-naked in front of your eyes. Cleanse the guilt from me!"

The gardener stands his ground proudly. Sweat covering his massive brown chest, he looks at her heaving breasts with appreciation.

Now *that's* race relations!

It's such a haunting scene, it made me tremble as I sat in the chair outside Coleman Hay's office.

The secretary got on the phone. Her head turned around to keep me from hearing she talked about someone being really depressed lately. I couldn't tell who it was, not that I gave a damn. The way she was turned, I could see the line of her body and it looked pretty good. Then I felt acid in my stomach, knowing Coleman Hay was probably nailing her.

I tried to keep calm, but my left arm started shaking and I couldn't keep my feet still. They kept wiggling. I knew she was going to turn around, see me all hyped-up and never let me in to see Coleman Hay. Only she kept talking on the phone, kept her back to me as the sweat poured down from my head. I licked it away from my lips and it tasted salty.

I closed my eyes again and waited.

#

I've been waiting here so long I'm completely drenched, but she doesn't look at me, so she doesn't notice.

The clock over her head says it's now two o'clock.

She's reading a magazine now. *Cosmopolitan.* Someone comes in and she looks up.

It's another blonde woman in a big hurry. A fur piece around her shoulders, this one's taller and skinner and waves at the secretary as she rushes right into Coleman's office.

The secretary shrugs and snaps her gum again. I hate that.

I'm thinking, maybe I'll shoot her first when a man comes in, so quickly and quietly I don't see him until he's past me. He's

big and wears a suit and looks a little like the guy who played
Schindler in the movie.

The secretary says, "Excuse me."

The man yanks Coleman Hay's chrome-metal door open,
slamming it against the wall on his way in.

The secretary rises, pushes her skirt down, snaps her gum
and sits again.

I'm definitely shooting her on my way out, if she's stupid
enough to still be here.

I hear loud voices coming from Coleman Hay's office. The
secretary looks up and someone shouts, "No! No!". Then gun
shots erupt in Coleman Hay's office, a bunch of shots. Eight I
think, or nine.

The secretary jumps up. I stand and reach around for the
Combat Masterpiece. The checkered grips are so wet, they're too
slippery to hold. I wipe my hands on the chair just as the door
crashes open again. The big guy moves through the doorway, a
large automatic pistol in his right hand.

He takes two steps toward the secretary, stops, raises the
gun to his temple and fires. He falls straight down and the
secretary screams and runs out. I pull out the Combat Masterpiece
and nearly drop it, it's so slippery. I hold it in a two-handed police
stance, bend my knees and move past the body and through the
doorway. I gotta make sure Coleman Hay's dead.

The blonde lies in front of the desk, her face a bloody pulp.
Coleman Hay is in his high-back chair behind his enormous black
lacquer desk. There are two holes in his forehead, a bloody mass
gobbed along the back of his chair. It's hardcore, man!

He's dead! I feel my heart stammering.

Then I hear voices outside.

I raise the Combat Masterpiece and aim it between
Coleman Hay's eyes.

The voices are right outside now.

I have to move quickly to the door, and ease behind it as it
opens. Two men rush in. I follow the swing of the door out, jump
over the big guy's body and walk right out without so much as

anyone even seeing me. I remember to uncock the Combat Masterpiece and slip it back under my shirt. There's a parking ticket on my windshield. I tear it up and toss it in the air.

I feel so good, I do a dance, a little jig next to my car. Then I see two police cars pull up and park haphazardly in front of the D.A.C., four officers rushing inside the building.

I'm no genius, but I'll bet Coleman was nailing the big guy's wife and got caught. Yep. That had to be it. I climb into my Datsun and pull away, resisting the urge to pump a few rounds into the police cars as I pass by. I catch a couple lights, still feeling pretty good, remembering the holes in Coleman Hay's head. I think, now the D.A.C. will get a new director and I'll finally see an opening night.

I weave through the streets, whistling. Then I get stuck in a traffic jam from hell on Decatur Street, so I turn up St. Louis, but it takes me nearly an hour to get to Rampart Street. I'm pissed again and hot as hell again and it occurs to me, what do I do now?

What if the next director doesn't see the light? What if he rejects my plays too? In my heart, I know he will. He'll be from uptown and drive a Mercedes and wear nice suits and hump blondes and only put on plays written by his friends.

What do I do? Go through all those rejections again, then kill him?

I think of the holes in Coleman Hay's head, but it doesn't give me the lift I'm looking for now.

I could . . . no . . . wow . . . I got it! I look out of my car window up at the sky. I've been inspired — a heavenly inspiration. I pull against the curb and sit there a minute, my hands shaking. My plan can still work.

What the hell was I thinking? Coleman Hay was nobody. I'm gonna kill somebody *famous*!

The Portrait of Lenore X

Come, let the burial rite be read — the funeral song be sung! —

An anthem for the queenliest dead that ever died so young —
Lenore by Edgar Allan Poe

"No, I haven't caught your murderer," John Raven Beau said, turning away from the balcony door to look at the portrait atop the dresser next to the fireplace. "I'm close," he told the portrait. "Very close."

The eight-by-ten inch, black-and-white photo stood in a gold-leaf wood frame. Beau studied the portrait again — the smooth white face, the high cheekbones, the full lips that appeared black from her dark lipstick; the small chin and straight black hair that hung below her shoulders — and the eyes. Her mesmerizing eyes, that seemed to stare at Beau no matter where he stood in the small apartment, were as dark as her hair.

Her unsmiling lips gave her mouth a sad look. Maybe she knew, when the portrait was taken a month ago, that she would be New Orleans's one hundred-and-tenth murder victim of the year and it was only May. Beau adjusted his belt to allow his nine millimeter Beretta to rest more comfortably on his hip. In a new light-weight black canvas holster, the Beretta rested on his right hip next to his gold star-and-crescent New Orleans Police detective's badge.

Beau stood six feet-two inches. His dark brown hair, nearly black, was as straight as the woman's in the portrait. His brown eyes were a shade lighter than hers. Sporting a two day's growth of beard, Beau wore a white dress shirt with black jeans and white tennis shoes. No suit today. It was Sunday, Beau's day off.

Beau turned back to the balcony's French doors, unlocked and opened them. Stuffy, the room smelled like old wood. A week ago a faint hint of the victim's perfume still lingered in the room. The air outside smelled heavy with rain. A fat drop of rain struck the window pane of the balcony door. Beau watched the rain move in, splatter against the glass pane as it came in waves across the red tile roofs of the French Quarter.

He took a step back, letting the mist flow over his face. Across Ursulines Street, the masonry walls of a Creole cottage became streaked with rain, the red brick walls of a three-story townhouse darkened, its black wrought iron balcony glistening in the sunshine.

"I guess the devil's beating his wife again," Beau told the portrait. "My dad told me if it rains while the sun is shining, Satan's beating his wife."

He looked at the mesmerizing eyes again and felt a tug at his heart. She was truly beautiful.

"The Quarter looks positively ancient in the rain," he told the portrait.

Leaving the doors cracked, Beau moved to the small double bed and sat on it. He ran his hand over the white brocade quilt and remembered how he first saw her, lying on her back in the bed with a neat wound over her heart. In his notes he'd written her name and age: Lenore Xavier. Twenty-two. Later, at the autopsy he'd written: Cause of death — penetrating gunshot wound to the heart. At the autopsy, the pathologist recovered a single .22 caliber pellet which he turned over to Beau to be sent to the Crime Lab for comparison to bullets from other unsolved murders. A knock at the door brought Beau back to the present.

He turned and looked at the varnished cypress door and said, "Come in." He knew who it was before the door opened.

A familiar round face peeked in at Beau. Wallace Flowright blinked his green eyes at Beau and stepped in. At six-feet tall, Wallace was a stocky man with red hair. A Tulane graduate student, 'a Ph.D. candidate' as he described himself to

Beau. He shoved his hands into his pockets and scraped the sole of his right shoe over the hardwood floor.

Looking sheepishly at his shoe, he said, "I heard someone walking up here. I figured it was you."

Wallace wore a green plaid shirt and tan slacks that were two sizes too tight along with brown deck shoes. Without looking up he added, "You've been here every day, haven't you?"

Beau pulled his ID folder from his right rear pocket and said, "If you're going to talk to me, I'll have to advise you of your rights again."

"Must you?" Wallace pulled his hands from his pockets and moved them back and forth like a second-grader standing in front of the principal. There was a strange look on the man's face, a hint of a smirk that didn't match the wide-eyed look to his eyes.

From his left rear pocket Beau pulled out an Olympus mini-tape recorder. He placed the recorder on the bed and turned it on, clipping its enhanced microphone to the brocade quilt. He looked at his watch and read the date and time into the recorder.

Beau dug a Miranda Warning card from his ID folder and began, "You have the right to remain silent . . ."

Wallace looked at him and swallowed hard. "Why haven't you arrested Carpenter?"

"Anything you say can and will be used against you in a court of law . . ." Beau continued until he finished the warning, then looked up at Wallace. "You understand these rights?"

Wallace nodded.

"The tape recorder can't hear a nod."

Wallace said yes, lowered his chin and said in nearly a whisper, "Why haven't you arrested Carpenter?"

"Carpenter was in Pass Christian the night of the murder. He has an ironclad alibi."

"But, I'm still a suspect?" The man's lips quivered.

Good, Beau thought as he nodded. Let him get emotional.

"You're still a suspect," he said.

Wallace took a step back, looked behind him and sat in the small wooden rocker next to the door. He began to rock. A gust of wind blew the French doors completely open. The white lacy curtains swished in the breeze. The room cooled immediately.

"Carpenter could have come here in the middle of the night. Shot her and left." Wallace spoke in a firm voice. "She never locked her door and you know the lock on the door downstairs is broken. He could have done it and gone back to Pass Christian."

Beau ran his hand over the quilt again. He wasn't sure, but he thought he caught a hint of her perfume again. He felt his heartbeat rising.

Getting back to Wallace, he said, "You knew she never locked her door too."

"Her door was always unlocked until you started coming here and locking it when you leave." Wallace stood up suddenly.

Beau watched him move to the foot of the bed and stare at the portrait. His hand shook as he raised it.

"Where did you get that?"

"Lenore's mother gave it to me."

Wallace narrowed his eyes at Beau and let out a gasp before he said, "Gave it to you? But . . . *you* never knew her."

"I'm the one who's going to catch her killer."

Wallace blinked as if he'd been slapped.

"But you never knew her."

"I know her very well." Beau looked at the portrait. "I dream about her every night." He waited a second before he added, "She ever visit you in your dreams?"

Wallace sat on the edge of the bed and stared at the portrait.

"Last night we went dancing," Beau said.

"At the policeman's ball?"

Beau shook his head. "You've seen too many old movies. There's no policeman's ball in New Orleans."

"Oh." Wallace continued to stare at the portrait.

"We went to a night club and did the Lambada and then slow danced. You ever Lambada?"

Wallace shook his head.

"It's very sexy. Very sensual."

Wallace blinked and a tear started down his round cheek.

Beau felt a smile crawling on his face. He stopped it immediately. Dropping his voice an octave, he said, "She wore a short red dress and red high heels. Gorgeous, man. There's nothing more beautiful as a brunette in a red dress."

He watched Wallace's chest rise and fall.

"You were a little in love with her, weren't you?"

"Everybody was," Wallace said in a high-pitched voice now. "She was . . ." His voice caught. He sucked in a deep breath and glared at Beau.

"You searched my apartment. Did you search Carpenter's? You ever find the murder weapon?"

"We searched his house and his car and his office."

Wallace shook his head in anger. He put his fists on his hips and said, "How old are you, anyway?"

"Thirty."

"I'm thirty too."

"I know." Beau looked around the room. "How long is your landlady going to leave the room like this?"

"What do you mean?" Wallace stood up and moved to the French doors.

"When is she going to rent it out again?"

Wallace shrugged. "What are you anyway, what nationality? You look foreign."

"I'm half Cajun and half Sioux."

"Sioux Indian? How did a Sioux end up in Louisiana?"

Beau was going to tell him how his mother married a solider, but opted for, "My family wouldn't stay on the reservation. That's why I became a cop."

"What?"

"I come from a family of trackers. The great Sioux trackers. My ancestors could track a man across anything."

Beau watched the man's Adam's apple move as he swallowed. Wallace slammed the French doors and pointed to a small puddle on the hardwood floor. He hurried into the bathroom and came back with a white towel.

"It's too soon to rent the apartment," Wallace said in a stronger voice. "Not with a murder here."

He went on his knees and wiped up the rain. He stood on shaky legs and looked at the portrait again.

Beau said in an even voice, "I know who did it."

Wallace took a step back. He wrung the towel in his hands and batted his eyes at Beau. "What?"

"I've eliminated every suspect. Except one."

Wallace stood very still.

"That's how we do it sometimes. Eliminate suspects until there's only one left. Then we stay on him until we have enough evidence."

Wallace sucked in a deep breath. "What evidence?"

"I can't tell you that. What I can tell you is . . . I know who did it. And I'll keep coming back until I prove it."

Wallace dropped the towel, picked it up and folded it and returned it to the bathroom. He came out with a nickel-plated .22 caliber Jennings model J-22 in his right hand. The hand quivered as he pointed the semi-automatic at Beau.

Beau smiled coldly. Standing, he said, "You're under arrest."

"I'll shoot you."

"No you won't. It's empty."

Sweat worked its way down the sides of Wallace's face.

Beau rubbed the stubble on his chin and moved toward Wallace. "We found the gun the night of the murder, right where you put it in the dirty clothes hamper. We took it to the lab and confirmed it was the murder weapon. No fingerprints, though. So I brought it back every time I came here and put it back in the hamper."

Stepping up to Wallace, Beau reached over and took the .22 from the wavering hand and shoved it into his left rear pocket. He pulled out his handcuffs tucked into his jeans at the small of his back and quickly cuffed Wallace behind the man's back.

He searched Wallace carefully. Wallace started crying.

Good! Beau led the man back to the bed and the recorder.

"I even know why you did it," Beau said.

"Huh?" Wallace shook his head and tried wiping the tears with his shoulders.

"You remember when I told you *why* isn't as important to us as *who, when, where,* and *how?"*

Wallace batted his eyes at him.

"Remember when I told you we don't need to prove motive?"

Wallace nodded now, slowly.

"The night before the murder, you came up here and found Carpenter asleep with her. Didn't you?"

The color left Wallace's face. "How . . . how'd you know?"

"Carpenter told me."

"He *saw* me?"

Beau felt it all fall into place, finally.

"She never seemed to see you, did she?"

Wallace gasped, his eyes misting again.

"She never really looked at you, did she? Like you were invisible to her."

Wallace bit his lower lip.

"So you took her away forever, didn't you?"

"You don't know. You don't know!" The man's face quivered, froth spat from his mouth. He gasped twice. "My heart . . . *hurt*. Every time I saw her. All the time!" Wallace dropped his chin and sobbed.

Beau stepped over to the dresser and took the portrait down and tucked it under his left arm. He picked the recorder up and waited for Wallace to stop bawling. He felt his own perspiration trailing down his back now. And again, he caught a whiff of Lenore's perfume. His heart raced.

Wallace stopped crying suddenly and focused his red eyes at Beau.

Beau put the mike in front of Wallace's face and said, "Is there anything else you want to add to your statement?"

Wallace coughed and said, "Go to hell!"

Beau checked his watch and read the time into the recorder and turned it off. He readjusted the portrait under his arm and Wallace reached for it.

"Let me see it." Wallace stared, bleary-eyed.

Beau slowly took the portrait and held it in front of Wallace and watched the man's eyes as they moved, as if the man was memorized the lines of her face, the length of her hair, her cheeks and chin and lips and eyes.

"I'll tell you," Wallace said, his voice trailing off. "I'll tell you all of it!"

Beau grabbed his elbow to guide him out.

"You can tell me the whole story at headquarters."

The D.A. loved a good confession.

Beau guided Wallace through the door into the hall.

"You're going to keep the portrait, aren't you?"

"It's mine." Beau said firmly. "Mine."

Except for the Ghosts

Sitting at an outside table at Café Du Monde, a table close to Decatur Street, Donald Tice waited for the woman he was going to kill.

He'd selected that particular table on a dry run the previous afternoon. From it, he could see Paula Lewis leave her antique shop, walk down Decatur to Madison Street and turn left for the small parking garage where she parked her car.

As the afternoon shadows crept across Jackson Square, Tice sipped his café-au-lait and waited. He felt the sun on his short-cropped blond hair, but it wasn't bothersome. He'd selected a light blue seersucker suit to wear because in New Orleans, the trick was to stay cool, especially in his business. His white shirt was cotton. He'd picked up his dark blue silk tie in Verona, Italy, on another job. His black Corfam shoes had rubber soles, the kind of shoes uniformed police officers wore, nearly as comfortable as sneakers. Clean-shaven, he looked like any other businessman.

He looked at his watch. Five-Thirty. He would kill Paula Lewis when she left work at six. Picking up the café-au-lait, Tice remembered what he knew of Paula — all he needed to know.

Part owner of Lovecraft Antiques, Paula was thirty, single, stood five-four, weighed about one hundred pounds, had long blonde-red hair, and drove a black Lexus.

On his dry run yesterday, Tice watched Paula walk to her car. She'd worn a yellow suit with matching high heels and walked without looking around, as most pretty women did. Only, as she passed across the street, she brushed her hair back with her hand and he got a good look at her face in profile. It took a full second to realize she looked so much like another woman, a woman he'd known so many years ago . . .

Picking up the paperback novel he'd bought at the airport, Tice pretended to read. He tried, but couldn't stop his mind from drifting back, back to another time here in New Orleans.

And he remembered the French Quarter in the rain . . .

A soft spring rain flowed over New Orleans, falling on the dark roofs of the Quarter, tumbling from the black, wrought-iron balconies, dancing on the narrow streets. Tice — no his name wasn't Tice then — he used his real name back then. He was Butch Johns and her name was Janet Grisham.

They stood beneath a lacework balcony, their backs pressed against the masonry wall of a Creole townhouse on Orleans Avenue. She stood close to him, her arms wrapped around his left arm, the smell of rain in her long reddish-blonde hair.

Janet looked at him with wild green eyes and winked seductively, the right leg of her wet jeans pressed against his leg. She pointed up the street and said, "Can you see them?"

"Who?"

"The ghost lovers."

She narrowed her eyes as she looked at the rainy street.

"I see a Frenchman with his lady walking toward the river. He's in a top hat and she's in a frilly gown." Pointing down the street, she said, "And here comes a Spaniard with a thin moustache and a dark-haired beauty hanging on his arm."

Butch squinted but couldn't see anything.

"Here comes a tall black man with a mulatto woman. He's in a gray tuxedo and she's in a white gown."

Butch closed his eyes and then cracked them open but still couldn't see the ghost lovers.

Janet pointed down Orleans and said, "Now we have a Sicilian with a handle-bar moustache. He's walking with a fair-skinned, dark-haired girl in a flowing green dress. And behind them comes an American couple, both with blonde hair, like us."

She snuggled again and closed her eyes.

"I can't see them," he said.

"You're not trying hard enough."

The rain continued and Butch realized how much older the Quarter looked in the rain, the streets wet and dark. Usually the Quarter was noisy, but that afternoon it was quiet and still, except for the rain.

"Don't you know," she said, "this city never runs out of lovers. Even the dead ones are still here."

Then suddenly the rain ended and the sun came out and it was steamy all over again in sub-tropical New Orleans. In the moments right after the rain let up, Butch narrowed his eyes and looked hard for the ghosts. He could barely see out of his eyes and after a while something fluttered in front of his eyes, like an old movie. He concentrated and finally saw shadowy figures moving along the streets — the Frenchman in a top hat and his woman in the frilly dress, the Spaniard with his dark-haired beauty, the black lovers in tuxedo and white gown, the Sicilians and the blonde American couple. In the moments right after the rain ended, the city seemed to hold its breath, and it felt as if everything stopped, except for the ghosts.

Tice's eyes snapped opened and he blinked the wetness away and looked at his watch. It was three minutes until six.

He reached down and patted the new .22 Walther PP in his coat pocket. He grabbed the coffee cup and raised it and his hand shook. His heart ached and his breathing was shallow; and he knew he'd better recover quickly.

He pushed the memories away, downing the remainder of the café-au-lait in one gulp. He didn't want to think about Janet now. That was twenty years ago. He'd walked out on her one morning, walked out — only to turn around a thousand times over the years looking for her, as if she'd be there, rushing after him.

Tice spotted Paula Lewis leaving work. She wore a black suit today with matching heels, a purse draped over her left arm. She looked straight ahead as she walked, her long hair bouncing.

Tice pushed his chair back started to stand, but his legs felt wobbly.

No, he thought, I can't be losing it.

It was all he had left. All he had was the precision of his work and the blessed months off between assignments. He tried to think of the aquamarine sea around Grand Cayman, where he'd spent his last rest period, before the letter arrived with the single sheet of description and a bad photo of Paula Lewis.

Then he remembered the last hit, how he'd missed with his first shot and had to chase his victim twenty yards before finishing him off.

Tice crossed the street and followed Paula in his rubber-soled shoes, his legs still jittery, his chest aching. As they turned the corner, he moved closer and started to withdraw the Walther when she turned and looked at him. He blinked and the Walther fell back in his pocket. His heart ached so much he thought it would explode.

Janet's face smiled sadly at him; but he knew it was Paula who'd turned to face him, a small nickel-plated Beretta .22 in her right hand. She pumped four quick ones into this chest, then dropped the pistol and hurried away. And he wondered, in that fleeting instant, what they *hadn't* told him about her.

Tice went down on his knees, reaching for her, and fell face forward.

"I don't want to die face down."

Struggling, he managed to roll over, the bullets burning deep in his chest, the coppery taste of blood on his tongue. Tice blinked up at the blue, cloudless sky and saw Janet's face hovering over him.

She was wet from the rain and her red lips glistened. She spoke to him but he couldn't hear her. Then, behind her, he saw the ghost lovers moving by, arm in arm, in the rain.

He reached up and touched Janet's arm and it was warm.

She pulled her long hair back with her right hand, leaned forward and kissed him. Her lips felt warm and tasted of rain. He was cold now and shivered as she pulled away. He tried to tell her he loved her, tried to tell her he always did. She smiled as if she knew. Then all was still, except for the ghosts moving behind her.

He felt his eyes closing and tried to keep them open.

Janet faded into darkness — a darkness so complete it engulfed him.

"I'm here, Darling," Janet said. "I'm right here."

He felt her next to him, felt her breath on his neck.

He looked up and saw they were passing beneath a lacework balcony.

This story is for debb

So Napoleon Almost Slept Here, Right?

New Orleans, 2027 A.D.

You'd think that when they cut off traffic through the French Quarter, when was that, back in 2015, they'd have stopped the goddamn busses. But no, they let those stink bombs keep barreling through so fat-assed conventioneers didn't have to waddle all the way from Canal Street to visit goddamn St. Louis Cathedral or stand in line to eat at Chef Jim LeBeau's or Antoine's.

One of those stink bombs nailed me, just as I crossed Chartres Street, before I could escape into The Napoleon House. It belched a shot of rancid smoke straight into my nostrils, causing me to sneeze twice as I wormed my way through the crowd at the entrance of the ancient cafe. I excused myself to a blue-haired lady, who turned her thin nose up in the air and looked away. She was wearing one of those all-in-one plasticine things that looked like a recycled garbage bag from a vintage television commercial. "Glad Bags," the actor called them. "Aren't you glad you use Glad?"

Easing up to the bar, which ran along the downtown side of the cafe, I waited until I could get the attention of the overworked bartender. While waiting, I gave the place the once over. It hadn't changed since I'd been in there a couple years earlier. Hell, like most places in the Quarter, it probably hadn't changed in centuries. Its stucco walls were littered with paintings of French scenes, and about a dozen portraits of Napoleon. There was also a large gray bust of Napoleon behind the bar.

The tender, a big man with a huge gut, moved my way and I finally caught his eye. He turned his wide face to me with a, "Yeah?"

"Excuse me," I said as I pulled out my creds and opened them so he could see my ID card and my star-and-crescent New Orleans Police badge. "I'd like to speak to the manager."

He scrunched up his beady eyes and said, "Say what?"

"I'd like to talk to the manager. Could you point me in the right direction?" *Come on*, I thought, *it's a simple damn question.*

The man's mouth contorted in a look of apathy as he raised his fat little arm and pointed toward the back of the place. I could see a door there. I thanked the tender and worked my way through the crowd. I knew the tender would continue watching me. It never ceased to amaze me just how easily people were thrown off by a polite cop, especially in New Orleans. I mean like, I didn't curse him or anything.

I caught a whiff of aroma from the kitchen just as I knocked on the door with the word *Private* on it. My stomach twitched at the strong scent of rich seasonings, probably gumbo or etouffee. A woman's voice behind the door said, "Come in."

She was sitting behind a wooden desk, and looked up at me with a flushed look on her face. Angry. Her dark green eyes taking a second to focus on me, revealing a hint of embarrassment at being caught in such a temper. Her brown hair, which had enough red highlights to cause an untrained eye to describe her as a red head, was parted down the center and pinned on the sides with barrettes, except for a unruly strand of hair that dangled in front of her left eye. She brushed back the strand of hair and shrugged, giving me one of those looks as if she was about to say something like, "When it comes to sex, men can't keep from lying and women can't keep from telling the truth." Of course, women never say that, except in old movies.

Moving her elbows to the top of her desk, she said, "What can I do for you?"

I pulled out my creds again and said, "I'm Detective Brouillette. Are you the manager?"

Standing, she extended her hand and said, "Heather Grayson." She had a nice handshake, firm, not one of those limp-wristed ones so in fashion nowadays. Moving around her desk, she told her computer to shut down and said to me, "Damn paperwork."

Now that I got a good look at her, I could see she was wearing one of those full dresses that went below the knees. Sleeveless, the dress had a low neck, which showed off her well-sculptured shoulders.

"I'm with the Unsolved Murder Squad," I said, loosening my tie with my right hand, pulling my MiniMac from my coat pocket. "Could I have a few minutes of your time?"

I told my computer to turn on. It was hot in the little office, very hot. Heather shot me a slight smile, one that said, "All right, if I have to, but this better be good because I would rather be running naked in a cool rain." I heard that line once, in a TV movie about the Carville Leper Colony.

"I'm investigating the murder of a man named Norman Moore, which occurred here at The Napoleon House ten years ago, in 2017. August 15th to be exact. At 11:20 p.m." I watched those green eyes widen slightly. "We're reopening the case," I explained. "Since your name isn't in the case file, I assume you weren't here then."

"Ten years ago, I was in Oregon." She had to brush the unruly strand from her eyes again. I liked that. Nothing like a good looking woman with a piece of herself that wouldn't listen.

I asked my computer for the names listed in the original murder report, then asked her about the lone eyewitness, a bartender named Keith Schitzmiffer.

"Are you making this up?" she said, putting a hand on her hip.

"No," I showed her the computer screen. She shook her head.

"Ain't much of a name," I admitted. Schitzmiffer was a pretty crappy name actually.

"No one here by that name."

"May I see you employee records?" I asked.

She shook her head again. "You know I can't show you that without a warrant or something."

I knew better, but I figured I'd try to charm her. She was eyeballing me pretty good. Obviously, there was a brain behind those emerald eyes. I liked that. I always liked my women smarter than me, which wasn't hard to find. The way I figure, show me a dumb woman and I'll show you someone faking. I rarely met one who couldn't outfox me. Except ole Eileen Brant. I could never convince her I wasn't a Private Eye. I told her I was the real police, must have showed her my badge fifty times, not to mention my uniform, hat, truncheon, police computer and departmental citations. Know what she said when I showed her my handcuffs? She asked if I had a second pair. Then she dropped her panties, climbed on my old brass bed and lay spread eagle. Sometimes, I do miss that girl.

Heather fanned the top of her dress and said, "It's hot in here." She eased around me and led the way back out into the cafe. Her dress might have been full, but I sure liked the way it hugged her hips when she walked in front of me. Sitting on a stool at the bar, she nodded to the tender, then turned back to me.

"What would you like?"

She had nice lips too, especially when pursed.

"Perrier," I said.

She told the fat tender, "Two."

I sat on the stool next to her.

"So," she said, "tell me about this murder."

"It was a Friday night. Two men were sitting over there," I pointed to the stools at the end of the bar, closest to Chartres Street. I told her how the men were drinking beer for about an hour. Then one of the men pulled out a small handgun and shot the other fella in the head and then walked out.

"The killer was in his early twenties, about 5'5", thin, with blond hair, wearing jeans and a black tee-shirt with the words, *Where the Hell is Eugene?* across the chest."

The tender put our drinks in front of us. I downed a deep gulp of the icy mineral water and felt better immediately. I was so hot. Putting my glass down, I added, "Police spent a week trying to find out where the hell this Eugene fella was."

She coughed up a mouthful of her drink all over the bar. I started to pat her on the back, but she turned away from me, pushing my hand away and grabbing a towel from the tender who had stepped up. She wiped her face and started to wipe the bar. Turning to me I could see her face was red. It took a couple second for her to catch her breath.

It took nearly half a minute before she could say, "Eugene's in Oregon."

"I know," I said. "The original detective who worked the case is an airport guard now."

I could see her eyes were wet now. When she started laughing, I felt a lot better. I took another hit of Perrier. Checking out the room again, out of habit, I noticed an angry looking man sitting at one of the tables. He was leering at me, giving me one of those Charles Bronson looks. He looked to be pushing fifty, with short gray hair. He was wearing a sleeveless tee-shirt, which showed off his tattoos. I could see a screaming eagle on his left shoulder. I leered back, just to prove a point and then asked the fat tender if he knew a Keith Schitzmiffer.

"He works around the corner at The Capdible Bar."

"Yeah?"

"He used to work here. Quit right after I started." The tender picked up the towel Heather had used.

I turned to Heather and she had an elbow up on the bar and was watching me. Twisted that way, the line of her body looked even sexier than before, her hip pointed toward me, her right breast pressed up against the back of her arm.

"Is there anyone still working here that was here in 2017?" I asked.

"No." The tender answered.

Heather nodded toward the tender. "He's been here longer than any of us."

I finished off my Perrier and thanked Heather and stood up.

"You really serious about a ten year old case?" Heather shot me a curious look, a little like the one Patricia Neal shot

Michael Rennie in *The Day The Earth Stood Still*, when he first told her about "Gort — Klatu, Barata, Nickto."

"Solved one last week that was twelve years old." I closed up my computer and tucked it back in my coat pocket.

"How?"

"Truth, like oil, will rise to the surface." I left her thinking about that line from an old Charlie Chan movie.

The Capdible Bar was a doghouse of a bar on Decatur Street, across from the Jackson Brewery Complex. If it wasn't in the goddamn Quarter, it would have been torn down a half century ago. But I'm sure the do-gooder preservationists would describe it as having, *atmosphere*. It had that all right, smelling like a well-used fire hydrant.

At least I didn't have to stay there long. The owner, a zorky looking punk with pink hair and a sunken chest named Robbie Tony, told me that Keith Schitzmiffer had the day off. I got Shitzy's address in LaCombe and started out the door.

"You should check The Napoleon House," the zork added. "Keith's girlfriend is a waitress there."

I waited until I was out on the banquette before calling back. "What's her name?"

"Sabrina. Little blonde with big tits."

Cute. Real Cute!

Heather was back in her office and the strand of hair was back in her face. I asked about Sabrina, and she took me into the side room of the cafe. Sabrina was serving a group of Japanese in the open air patio. I watched her for a minute. She was the impatient type, obviously annoyed at the politeness of the small foreigners.

Heather took Sabrina aside, passed her order pad to one of the prim gay waiters and asked the waitress to take a break. "I'll be back in my office," Heather told me before leaving us.

I pulled out my computer and started in on my interview. Her name was Sabrina Nash and she'd worked there for five years. She and Keith had lived together for four years. "He's at home," she explained, giving me the phone number and address. I took mental notes: Pushy. Aggravating.

She wasn't a bad looking girl with white blond hair and an oversized chest and blue eyes. She said she was thirty. She reminded me of that little blonde woman in that old movie *The Getaway* with Steve McQueen. Sally something.

"Has Keith ever told you about the murder that occurred here?"

Sabrina, who was standing next to the spiral staircase in the patio, put her arm up on the banister and nodded slowly. She wasn't looking in my eyes when I asked that question, but gave me a hard look as soon as I did.

"What did he tell you?"

"Said he was tending bar. There were two guys drinking and talking at the bar. One of them pulled out a pistol, put it against the other guy's ear and fired. Then the killer picked up his glass and left. That's why y'all didn't find any fingerprints."

"What did Keith say the killer looked like?"

Sabrina had the description down pat, and she hadn't read the computer file that morning.

"Nobody ever saw him again." Yawning, she covered her mouth before adding, "There was a lot of blood."

"I guess it's etched in your boyfriend's mind."

"Like it was yesterday."

I had one more question. I asked where she was ten years ago. She said Iowa. When I asked her what town, she laughed at me. She meant Iowa, Louisiana. Real cute. I knew that one-dog town. Didn't even have a Walmart.

I gave Sabrina my card and told her I'd talk to Keith when he got back to work tomorrow. On my way to thank Heather, I spotted the angry Charles Bronson clone, still at the same table, still glaring at me.

I thanked Heather and gave her a card. Smiling, she said she had a question.

"How tall are you?"

"Six-three."

"You look taller."

"It's the bulk." My mother calls me thick-bodied, my father, heavy-set. I'm just big all over, even my hands, even my toes. I'm thirty-three now and still have never met anyone with bigger toes. My claim to fame.

I passed her one of my cards and she passed me hers, which was on parchment paper:

Heather Grayson
General Manager

THE NAPOLEON HOUSE CAFE

500 Chartres Street   New Orleans
Phone 524-7522-9177

Looking at my card, she said, "Bye Max" She used the same voice Elizabeth Taylor used on Van Johnson in *The Last Time I Saw Paris*. I hate my first name, even when a good looking woman uses it while flirting. Max Brouillette . . . *Jesus!*

On my way out, I passed Charlie Bronson. I placed my hands on his table, leaned toward his ear and whispered, "Quit eyefucking me, ass-hole!"

It was the second time that day I caused someone to cough up a mouthful. Wiping his drink from the front of his shirt, the angry man stood up quickly. I braced myself, preparing to tattoo the old fucker with a right hook.

The man scrunched up his face and snarled at me, "You goddamn detectives are so stupid."

I waited for the next brilliant statement.

"Think you gonna solve that old case? No way."

I narrowed my eyes. He looked older up close, had to be pushing sixty. His breath reeked of gin and bingara.

Still rubbing his wet shirt, he said, "I'm Wellesley. Art Wellesley. Check me out. I used to be N.O.P.D."

It was my turn to back up. I unclenched my right fist and had to ask, "What's your problem?"

"I hate cops." With that, he sat down and went back to his drink.

He continued eyeballing me right out of the place. I watched him as I walked away, but was immediately distracted by another stink bomb that belched on me as I walked along the St. Louis Street side of The Napoleon House. Moving away, I felt just like Bogie must have, when he walked out of the Sternwood Mansion the first time in *The Big Sleep.*

The next afternoon, I was surprised to see no busses on Chartres. I paused a moment across the street and took a good look at The Napoleon House. Three stories tall, the masonry facade had peeled away in places to reveal the red brick and timber construction. The building was as gray as one of those old time battleships. Next to the front door were several bronze plaques, explaining how some batwing Nineteenth Century mayor of New Orleans planned to rescue Napoleon Bonaparte from that prison island and bring him to town, to live out his twilight years. Only the emperor died before they got to rescue him.

The same fat tender was behind the bar. Art Wellesley was at the same table. The only thing that changed was the color of his tee-shirt. I watched him as I moved straight to Heather's Office. Earlier, at my office I had discovered Wellesley had been fired for shooting a K-9 officer after the officer's dog bit Wellesley. He shot the officer in the leg. A routine gunshot wound, the man developed a serious infection in the hospital and lost his leg. Goddamn doctors.

Heather wasn't in her office. The tender told me she was probably upstairs.

"What's there?"

"She lives on the second floor. She's taking a quiet lunch break."

So I went over to The Capdible Bar and was slapped with a nice surprise. The zorky owner blinked at me with confused eyes. "Haven't you heard?"

"Heard what?"

"Keith Schitzmiffer's dead. He OD'd last night."

Now if there's one thing a good homicide man didn't believe in . . . it's *coincidence.* I shot straight back to The Napoleon House. I wasn't too surprised to find Sabrina wasn't in, figuring she had funeral arrangements. So I waited at the bar for Heather to come down.

A half hour later she waltzed in wearing a short pink dress, one of those breezy semi-sheer things with straps around back. She had curled her hair and was wearing darker lipstick and looked good enough to eat. I followed her into her office and liked the way she smiled at me when she turned around and saw me in the doorway.

"I need a little privacy. Mind if I call my office from in here?"

She moved from behind her desk and said, "My pleasure," offering me her chair. I could see she wasn't wearing a bra. I tried not to leer at the outline of her breasts as I moved around her desk. Heather started to leave but I called her back. "I don't need privacy from you." She sat in the only other chair in the office, a stuffed chair in the corner next to the door. I watched her cross her legs.

I instructed my MiniMac to contact the LaCombe Police. When it beeped, I asked LaCombe for the case officer of the Schitzmiffer Case. Heather stood up and cupped her right hand in the form of a glass and pointed outside. I watched her hips as she walked out. It wasn't as hot in there as yesterday. And today, Heather's perfume lingered in the air, sweet and sexy.

Three minutes later, when a window opened on my MiniMac, I watched the video image of the LaCombe officer who'd just handled the Schitzmiffer cadaver. I had everything I needed to know by the time Heather came in with two icy Perriers.

"Keith Schitzmiffer's dead," I told her.

"What?" Her surprise was genuine. She sat back down.

"He overdosed on Blixen." Which was easy to do. They didn't call it the indigo devil for nothing.

"So, what do you do now?"

"Sabrina," I told her. Then I told her about coincidences and right in the middle of taking another gulp of Perrier, it hit me, like a slap across the face. Heather saw it in my eyes and sat up.

"What is it?"

I felt a smile creep across my face. I turned to the side and told my computer to get me everything it could on Sabrina Nash. "Check every data base," I told it. It took about ten seconds and, as usual, disappointed me. Never arrested, Sabrina had reported herself the victim of a crime only once, a purse snatching on Canal Street. She had traffic ticket and a valid driver's license. But sometimes, the lack of information can tell you a lot. Sabrina Nash never had electricity or gas or a telephone in her own name. Ever.

Taking another sip of Perrier, I asked Heather, "How about dinner tonight?"

"I'm working until midnight," she answered before finishing off her Perrier. "But we can go for coffee now, if you'd like."

I liked. I tucked my computer back into my coat and got up. Heather went out first and told the fat tender she'd be away for a few minutes. I was exchanging looks with Charlie Bronson Wellesley when I had another surprise. Sabrina Nash strolled in at that moment and waved to Heather on her way out to the patio.

Heather shot me a quizzical look and I raised my hand, tapped my watch and flashed five fingers at her. She nodded and climbed up on the stool. I pulled my eyes away from her legs and followed Sabrina out into the patio amongst the banana trees and palms and the black, wrought iron tables. Next to the kitchen, it smelled of boiled crabs.

Sabrina didn't look upset at all, until she realized I was standing behind her. She had made her face up pretty good and was wearing a shorter than usual skirt.

I smiled at her, excused myself and asked how she was doing. She said fine, under the circumstances. Then I asked her to repeat the story Keith Schitzmiffer had told her about the killing. She gave me a "pshaw" and repeated it verbatim.

Then she said, "Don't you wanna know about how I found Keith this morning?"

"Naw," I said, inching closer with my MiniMac. Sometimes that little bastard can be pretty intimidating. Especially when I ask official questions and its lights flicker as it records everything. Sabrina was looking right at it when I asked my next question.

"Would you sign a waiver for your medical files for me?"

She looked at me as if I'd just reached over and pinched her tit. Then her blue eyes narrowed. She moved around me and went into the cafe. I followed and found her standing next to Heather, her hands on her hips.

"If you're going to allow the police to question me at work, I want a union official present."

"That won't be necessary," I said, reaching around for Heather's hand. "I have no more questions for you."

Sabrina gave me a hard stare.

"Just don't leave town," I told her. "It'd be foolish of you to try."

As soon as we got outside, Heather asked, "Can you do that? Make her stay in town."

"Naw. It's a line from an old movie named *Laura*. It was what Dana Andrews, the detective with the silver shinbone from the Siege of Babylon, told Vincent Price, the sleazy boyfriend.

I took Heather down Chartres to la Madeleine French Cafe on Jackson Square. We grabbed two mugs of coffee-and-chicory and sat against a window along the St. Peter Street side of the cafe, which smelled wonderful. The cafe smelled of fresh baked bread. No way I could sit there and not eat something. I went back to the counter for a couple almond croissants.

I would have rather eaten Heather, and was thinking about just that as she sat across from me, sipping her coffee, breaking off small pieces of croissant to place on her tongue, shooting smiles at me occasionally as I watched her. There's something about a pretty girl lips when she purses them to take a sip of . . . anything.

I stared at this girl as she picked at my brain. I heard myself explaining about homicides, how the initial twelve hours of a murder were the most critical and how I was up against a brick wall, but how much I loved that challenge. She asked something about the crime scene, about what evidence we'd secured. I told her how a victim dies once and a crime scene is murdered a hundred times. "Physical evidence ain't all it's cracked up to be," I heard myself say. "Unless you catch the killer and can match the pieces."

Then I told her how everyone lies. How murders lie because they have to, how witnesses lie because they think they have to. Then I told her the secret to solving old murders.

"People forget the lies. They only remember the truth. You just have to ask the right questions."

She looked at me as if she thought I was smart. I liked that. We had a second cup before leaving. It was dark by then and much cooler. So we took a leisurely stroll around Jackson Square and across Decatur Street. Except for the goddamn mimes, it would have been perfect, especially when Heather tucked her arm in mine.

We crossed over the sea wall to the Moonwalk. I tried to be nice to a mime who was mimicking a blind man and managed to send him on his way without having to drop kick him across the river.

We sat on a wooden bench along the boardwalk and looked at the river, at the lights reflecting on the dark water, at a large ship silently passing on its way to the gulf. It was a gorgeous night. Heather leaned her head against my shoulder and I thought of another old movie, a Woody Allen movie. Woody was sitting on a bench with a pretty girl, overlooking the Hudson River. What was her name? Annie Hall? No, I remember the movie's title was *Manhattan*. Yeah, I was feeling pretty good until the gun blast.

I felt it strike the bench even before my ears told me we were under fire. I shoved Heather down and jumped on her, withdrawing my weapon as another shot rang out. It sounded like a handgun, an old gunpowder model. I waited for three seconds before rising slowly.

Nothing. Not even a shadow stealing away in the darkness. I found two other couples along the boardwalk, but as usual, no one saw anything. With Heather's nervous hand in mine, we walked back to The Napoleon House, my right hand in my coat pocket, cradling my new Smith and Wesson Stun 7.

"Hey," I told the tender. "Did Sabrina leave?"

"Naw. She's in the back."

I peeked in the back and sure enough, Sabrina was serving two couples, all wearing cowboy hats.

"Did she leave while we were gone?" I asked the tender.

"What am I, her mother?"

"I need a drink," Heather said as soon as we eased up to the bar. She ordered a Sazerac from the fat tender. I got a scotch rocks. It felt much cooler in the cafe and the strong liquor helped me down from the night's excitement. That was until Heather bumped me with her hip, focused those dark greens on me and said, "Let's go upstairs."

I followed those nice hips up the spiral staircase to her room where she left the door open and moved in the semi-darkness ahead of me. I closed the door and flipped on a small lamp in the living room of her apartment. Heather stopped in the doorway to her bedroom and began to unfasten the straps along the back of her neck. I felt my heartbeat pounding in my ears.

I moved over and helped her, letting my fingers roll down her shoulders to the small of her back as her dress fell to the floor. My fingers worked their way down into the elastic band of her panties as she craned her neck back and kissed me, gently on the lips. I turned her around and kissed her good and hard, French kissed her as my oversized hands caressed her breasts and rubbed her hard nipples. I felt her hand at my crotch.

How we managed to stop long enough to get our clothes off is beyond me, but we did and moved, naked to her bed. In that brief moment, Heather said in a gasping voice, "I sure hope you have a current health card."

    I stepped back to my clothes and dug out my creds, opened
them and pulled out my health card, which I'd updated a week
earlier. That's right, no communicable diseases.
    Heather was sitting on her bed, cross legged, her health
card in hand.
    "I updated it yesterday," she said. "After I met you." I put
both cards on her night stand and climbed next to her.
    Okay, so I'm an old fashioned southern boy. So I'm not
going to explain all the sweaty, steamy details. Let me put it this
way, I think there was an earthquake in downtown New Orleans
that night. Well, it sure moved for me. Lying there, in a post
intercourse snuggle, I remembered another line from Charlie Chan
. . . "Love is as unexpected as squirt from aggressive grapefruit."
    Sure, this wasn't love, at least not yet. But the squirting
was good.
    I felt myself dozing and fought it. Typical male. I opened
my eyes and saw Heather staring at me. She kissed me again and
asked if I wanted a drink. I told her no.
    "How about seconds?"
    The second time around was longer and harder and hotter
and she came twice before I climaxed. She continued kissing me
as I rolled off her and lay there. Heather rested her head on my
chest and soon, I felt the world slipping away.
    When I woke, the clock said it was two in the morning.
Heather was cradled against me in a fetal position. I watched her,
watched her chest rise and fall in easy breaths. She slept with her
mouth open and her hair was messed over her face and she looked
beautiful. Snuggling with her, I remembered how The Sundance
Kid described the woman he wanted, "I'm not picky, long as she's
smart, pretty, sweet, gentle, tender, refined, lovely . . . "
    When I woke again, it was daylight. The clock read nine
o'clock. Heather, still naked, was sitting up in bed next to me. She
was sipping coffee. That's what woke me, the strong scent of
coffee.
    "On the table," she nodded. My cup was on the end table,
and just the way I liked it, cream and two sugars. I sat up and took

a gulp. Heather had put a touch of make-up on her face, not that
she needed it. She smiled at me wickedly.

I leaned back against the head board and looked around.
"So, Napoleon almost slept here, huh?"

"No," she answered, pulling that runaway strand of hair
from her eyes once again. "There's a room down the hall. It's
called L'Appartement. You should see the place. It's like a
museum. That's where he was supposed to stay, after the break
out."

I took another hit of coffee. Heather, running her fingers
through her hair said, "What is it? Why are you smiling like that?"

Seeing her sitting like that in the daylight, cross-legged and
naked and sexy as hell, made me smile like that. I finished my
coffee, climbed out of bed and asked if she'd have dinner with me.
She said she'd think about it. Rising, she grabbed my hand and
lead me to the shower.

I know, this is supposed to be a murder mystery. So I'll get
back to it. After the long hot shower, I went straight to the
Moonwalk and called the crime lab and dug out a pellet from the
wooden bench. I sent it to the firearms examiner. Before I
finished my second cup at la Madeleine, I got a call on my
MiniMac. I bet you can guess what the message on my screen
said.

That's right. The pellet from the Moonwalk was fired from
the same pistol that killed Norman Moore at The Napoleon House
ten years ago, in 2017. August 15th to be exact. At 11:20 p.m.

Four hours later, armed with a search warrant, I crossed
Chartres Street again, right behind a belching bus that didn't bother
me in the least. Accompanied by two patrolmen, I marched
through The Napoleon House, straight to the office door and
knocked on it. Heather answered. She was wearing a yellow dress
with a frilly top. I explained before starting my search, explained
that I'd just come from LaCombe where I'd searched the
Schitzmiffer/Nash apartment, and how we were holding Sabrina at
headquarters.

Thirty-seven minutes after beginning my search, the fat
tender, who had been shadowing me, pointed to something that
didn't belong behind the bust of the Emperor Napoleon that stood
behind the bar, against the long mirror. It was a small box. In the
box was a Davis .32 caliber, chrome plated pistol with laminated
wood grips. That's right. A piece of shit.

I called the crime lab and waited for them to come for the
gun. I had a Perrier with Art Wellesley. He didn't like my
company much, but I couldn't resist. Leaning over, I told him I'd
just solved that old murder.

"Bullshit!"

I leaned closer and gave him a line from *Blazing Saddles*.
"You bet your ass."

I winked at Heather before leaving. She held one hand to
her ear and played like she was punching numbers on a phone with
the other. I nodded.

Charlie Chan once said, "Silence is golden . . . except in
police station."

Sabrina Nash was waiting for me handcuffed to a chair in
an interview room. When I came in with two cups of coffee, she
stuck out her chin in defiance. It took a while, but before we
stepped out of that interview room, three hours and three cups of
coffee later, her head was bowed and my MiniMac contained a
detailed murder confession.

Sabrina's blue eyes remained hard, even when confessing.
But I'll never forget how they blinked in haunted recognition when
I gave her the weenie. I slipped it to her softly. She didn't even
recognize it as the weenie at first, even when I showed her how
Keith Schitzmiffer had explained the killing to the first officers on
the scene and again in his formal statement early the next morning
to detectives. "He placed the gun against the man's temple and
shot him." Keith said nothing about the ear. He said temple.
Sure, the autopsy report described the wound as . . . "Penetrating
gunshot wound of the right ear canal."

It had been the word "ear" that had rattled around in my head after I first talked to Sabrina. That was the weenie. I asked her, "How did you know about the ear?"

"Only the killer, the police and the coroner knew about the ear," I told her. Grinning, I added the kicker, "But even we didn't know about the glass. There were so many glasses on the bar, no one realized the killer had taken the glass, except you."

She wouldn't look me in the eye and I knew it was a just matter of time, especially after the crime lab came back with her fingerprint on the Davis .32.

"You found it?" she said. She was actually surprised. *Jesus!* Thank God criminals are stupid.

I sat back and told her the exact opposite. I told her she was one smart girl, told her how she'd out foxed us, told her we'd have never caught her if it wasn't for luck. Then I asked her, if she'd just do me the enormous favor, and tell me how she'd disguised herself that night, ten years ago.

When she told me she was a sex change, I acted surprised as hell, even though I'd already had a warrant ready for her medicals. Sabrina's transformation was a good one. Usually I can tell by the hips. Sex changes have thin, male hips. She looked every bit a female. Too bad they couldn't transform the brain. She still had a male brain.

She never boned up to what really happened to Keith Schitzmiffer. But what the hell? No case is perfect, except in the movies. I did get to laugh at the fat tender when my partners brought him into the Detective Bureau. I charged him as an accessory to attempt murder of a police officer.

Before I stepped out of the Detective Bureau, Sabrina had a question for me. "Don't you want to know why I went back to The Napoleon House?"

I looked into those blue-blue eyes and said, "Because it was your greatest moment."

I called Heather before walking Sabrina over to Central Lockup. She wanted to know everything.

"I'll tell you over dinner. Pick you up in an hour?"

"We're eating here," she said. "In L'Appartement. Then we're gonna make love on Napoleon's bed."

I liked that.

Okay, so you're thinking this wasn't much of a case, wasn't much of an investigation. So let me feed you another old homicide cliché.

"It's good to be good. But it's better to be lucky."

Just call me lucky. I hate the name Max.

This story is for debb

The End

O'Neil De Noux

Illustration © Dana De Noux

O'Neil De Noux writes realistic crime fiction featuring the accurate dialogue of the street and strong settings, primarily New Orleans. He also writes breath-taking erotica and science fiction adventure stories in the vein of Edgar Rice Burroughs. His publishing credits include seven novels, five short story collections and over two hundred short stories published in multiple genres.

De Noux's published novels include *GRIM REAPER*, *THE BIG KISS*, *BLUE ORLEANS*, *CRESCENT CITY KILLS*, *THE BIG SHOW, MAFIA APHRODITE* and *SLICK TIME*. *THE BIG KISS* was translated into Swedish and published in Sweden in 2006, under the title *TVÅ HÅL I HUVDET (TWO HOLES IN THE HEAD)*. His short story collections include *NEW ORLEANS MYSTERIES*, *HOLLOW POINT/THE MYSTERY OF ROCHELLE*

MARAIS and *LaSTANZA: NEW ORLEANS POLICE STORIES*, which received an "A" rating from *ENTERTAINMENT WEEKLY MAGAZINE*. De Noux adapted one of the *LaSTANZA* stories "Waiting for Alaina" into a screenplay, which was filmed in New Orleans and broadcast on local TV in 2001.

In March 2006, *NEW ORLEANS CONFIDENTIAL,* a collection of 1940's noir private-eye short stories was published by Point*Blank* Press. From *Publisher's Weekly*, 3/13/06: "Former homicide detective De Noux turns out an engaging, fast-paced collection of stories featuring private eye and womanizer extraordinaire Lucien Caye as he tracks philandering husbands, possible murderers and missing cats. Set predominantly against the rich backdrop of 1940s New Orleans, these stories-abounding with ample bosoms and willing women-are fun, and the author knows his stuff when it comes to the Big Easy."

A Lucien Caye story, "The Heart Has Reasons" (which appeared in *Alfred Hitchcock Mystery Magazine*'s September 2006 Issue), won the Private Eye Writers of America's prestigious *2007 Shamus Award* for *Best Short Story*. The *Shamus* is given annually to recognize outstanding achievement in private eye fiction. In 2009, the Short Mystery Fiction Society awarded the *Derringer Award* for *Best Novelette* to another Lucien Caye story, "Too Wise" by O'Neil De Noux (which appeared in *Ellery Queen Mystery Magazine*'s November 2008 Issue). The *Derringer Award* is given annually to recognize excellence in the mystery short form.

In May 2006, *NEW ORLEANS IRRESISTIBLE*, a collection of erotic detective stories by O'Neil De Noux, was published by EAA Signature Series Books. *AMERICAN CASANOVA – The New Adventures of the Legendary Lover*, A Collaboration of 15 Writers Directed by Maxim Jakubowski was also published in 2006 (Avalon Publishing, New York). A non-fiction book, *SPECIFIC INTENT*, was a lead title from Pinnacle Books and a main selection of the Doubleday Book Club. This true-crime book details the intricate police investigation of a murder case which shocked south Louisiana.

O'Neil De Noux's short stories have been published in the U.S., Canada, Denmark, England, France, Germany, Greece, Italy, Japan, Portugal, Scotland, Sweden and Ukraine. From 1993 to 2005, De Noux taught creative writing and mystery writing at Tulane University, University of New Orleans and Delgado Community College. After Hurricanes Katrina and Rita, De Noux taught creative writing at McNeese State University, Lake Charles, LA. He is the founding editor of two fiction magazines, *MYSTERY STREET* and *NEW ORLEANS STORIES*.

O'Neil De Noux has worked as a homicide detective and organized crime investigator. He has also been a private investigator, U.S. Army combat photographer, criminal intelligence analyst, newspaper writer, magazine editor, computer graphics designer. As a police officer, De Noux received seven commendations for solving difficult murder cases. In 1981, he was named 'Homicide Detective Of The Year' for the Jefferson Parish Sheriff's Office. In 1989, he was proclaimed an 'Expert Witness' on the homicide crime scene in Criminal District Court, New Orleans, LA. Mr. De Noux is a graduate of Archbishop Rummel High School in Metairie, LA, Alabama's Troy University, and The Southern Police Institute of the University of Louisville, KY (Homicide Investigation).

After his home was seriously damaged by Hurricane Katrina, O'Neil De Noux re-settled on the northshore of Lake Pontchartrain in 2006 and returned to law enforcement. He is currently a Police Investigator with the Southeastern Louisiana University Police Department in Hammond, LA. In 2008, De Noux was awarded the department's highest decoration, the *Chief's Award of Excellence* for outstanding service.

In September 2009, O'Neil De Noux received an Artist Services ***Career Advancement Award for 2009-2010*** from the Louisiana Division of the Arts for work on his forthcoming historical novel set during The Battle of New Orleans.

Made in the USA
Lexington, KY
15 July 2011